Mindset

by Stephen Sadler

Mindset is published by Folktellers Studios LLC

Paperback ISBN 978-0-9830161-2-0

SAN 859-9963

Printed in the United States of America

10 9 8 7 6 5 4 3 2 1

I dedicate this book to my wife Laurie and my children, who have always supported me.

My eternal love.

From The Author

Over the last 30 years, I have spent a majority of my time inventing and building products, software, and technologies. Recently, I came to a point in my life where I still loved inventing and creating, but I was tired of having to make things work and keep them operational. Interestingly enough, writing has become my release. When I write, especially sci-fi stories, I still feel the same reward of invention and creation; however, I don't have to build a prototype, or even write one line of code. As matter of fact, after the research is done, all I have to do is explain it, say it works, and magically all the technology in the story works, just because I said it did! Obviously, this is far easier than conceiving an idea, patenting it, building a business and marketing plan, procuring sales and investment, and so on, and so on. Seriously though, I really love to write, and the older I get, the more it seems like my passion.

We all know many concepts and ideas born in sci-fi can become reality. So I hope this book will help to slow down evil usages of future ideas and inventions. However, based on history, I doubt it.

Mindset – Abaddon has many parallels to my own life that are very close to my heart. I really hope you enjoy the story. Stephen Sadler

Mindset

Prologue

The heat was intense as Matthew McConnell jogged out of the tunnel onto the Stratham College football field for the first game of the 1989 season. Stratham hadn't had a winning season in Texas for ten years, so the stands were only half full. Even the marching band looked unorganized and unengaged.

McConnell was 5 feet 10 inches, medium athletic build, with dirty blond hair and blue eyes. Growing up just outside of Dallas, he had a strong Texas accent. McConnell was only a sophomore, but in his mind, he was the team's best quarterback. He hated living within the shadow of his nemesis, the starting quarterback and senior, Phil Green. He envied him with every bone in his body, and his resentment grew every time his team lost another game.

"Why does Coach like this idiot? He's absolutely worthless," he said to one of his teammates as he moved in front of the large cooling fan.

"Don't know McConnell, I'm not Coach. I'm sure you'll get a shot one of these days," his teammate replied.

"Well, I'm glad I'm not playing today; it's hotter than hell out here," he said. McConnell knew that wasn't the truth; he wanted the starting QB position so bad he could taste it. He didn't even appreciate his athletic scholarship, although it paid for his entire education. McConnell watched from the sideline as Stratham won the coin toss and elected to receive the ball.

Here goes another losing season, he thought as he watched Barkley's kicker hammer the ball deep into their end zone.

"Take a knee," McConnell shouted. However, the kickoff returner decided to run it out. "No, what is he doing?" Quickly, the kickoff returner was tackled at the 7-yard line.

What an idiot. Is everyone on this team brain dead? he thought.

As the teams switched, he watched Phil Green take the field.

This should be good for a laugh, McConnell thought. *We haven't beaten Barkley since 1980.*

Green barked out the count, "BLUE 22, RED 80, HUT HU..." but before he could finish the count, the center snapped the ball. Green, who wasn't ready, fumbled the exchange and dove on the ball, nearly losing possession. As Green peeled himself off the ball, McConnell shook his head in total disgust.

"I see this season is not going to be any different," he remarked, leaning over toward a couple of teammates.

As he looked back at the field, the second play was

already on the go. Green rolled right, stepped out of the pocket and threw the ball at least three yards behind Stratham's new star tight end, Rob LaVie, causing it to nearly get picked off by the defense.

"Come on, Green, try to keep the ball out in front of him," McConnell yelled, and Green scowled back at the sideline as he walked into the huddle. Stratham lined up for the third play.

"GREEN 40, RED 80, HUT," barked Green and quickly rolled out of the pocket with LaVie wide open 30 yards down the field. However, instead of passing, Green foolishly kept running and was tackled five yards short of the first down marker.

"What the hell are you doing? You had LaVie wide open," screamed McConnell.

Hearing McConnell, Coach Francis turned around and warned him, "Keep it positive, son, or you'll never see the field again."

"Yes, Coach," replied McConnell putting his head down. At that moment, LaVie came off the field and stood beside him in front of the cooling fan. LaVie was slender, 6 feet 2 inches and the type of athlete who seemed to have superhuman strength and agility.

"Is Green blind? You were wide open, LaVie," said McConnell, who was more interested in Green's failure than watching their defense.

"Yep, do you think you could do better?" said

LaVie as he removed his helmet. He was good looking; however, his white pigmentation and dark piecing eyes gave him a devious appearance.

"Of course, my grandmother could have done better than Green," replied McConnell confidently and arrogantly. "But we both know that's never going to happen. Coach loves Green."

"We'll see, Mac. I have this feeling you're going to do great things over your career," he smiled with an odd sparkle in his eye.

"My career? What do mean?" asked McConnell.

"Well, my new friend, sometimes in life, all you need is a little help to open a window of opportunity," said LaVie, then he laughed. As the Stratham punt return team came off the field, LaVie put on his helmet and said, "And your window is just about to be opened." With that, he jogged onto the field.

Mac watched on, as LaVie walked over to Green and whispered something into his ear. Green nodded back in agreement, and they both entered the huddle.

"OK, 686 Pump F-Stop - on three," said Green. They clapped and lined up on the line of scrimmage. Green looked over at LaVie as if to change the play on the fly.

"RED80, RED80, HUT, HUT, HUT" barked Green. Mac watched intently, wondering what LaVie had said to Green.

What's he up to? Mac thought.

As the ball was hiked, LaVie didn't run the 6 route. Instead, he came back across the field behind Green, obviously looking for a hand-off from their trick play. At the same time, the fullback stopped and moved backwards to block. As the play developed, the fullback stepped directly on Green's foot, causing Green to twist directly into LaVie's path. Within an instant, LaVie hit Green at full speed, knocking him backwards while the fullback still had Green's foot planted firmly on the turf. Even from the sideline you could hear Green's leg break and the shriek of his pain. He then lay there in silence and in shock.

As the medics came onto the field and attended to Green, LaVie walked slowly past McConnell and seemed to glow with a wicked look of satisfaction.

"McConnell, you're in," yelled Coach Francis.

Chapter One

Jack and Grace Cooper sat quietly on the front porch of their Cape Cod-style Michigan home. The sun was about to set, and the air was warm for late September. It was one of those few moments in life where everything felt perfect. With her head on his shoulder, they both remained perfectly still, watching and listening to the neighborhood kids kicking a soccer ball at the house across the street. Both remembered when their daughter Emma played soccer at that age and wondered where all the time had gone.

As Jack looked over at Grace, he thought, *It's 2016 already, wow. I still remember when Emma started kindergarten in 2000. Y2K, what a crazy year for technology that was.* He laughed silently.

Ever since he graduated University of Michigan, he had a passion for inventing and commercializing new types of medical technologies. Over the last few years he had invented several software and hardware applications for the field of neurotechnology. The problem was he had a bad habit of starting more projects than he could afford, which had placed a financial strain on the family at times.

Jack was 5 feet 10 inches, with a fairly athletic build from years of playing ice hockey in Michigan's beer leagues. He hated the stereotype that geeks couldn't be athletes, and he did almost everything to break that mold.

As he looked over at his wife, he noticed how beautiful she still was, and he smiled.

Suddenly breaking the silence and startling Grace, his smartphone produced a loud tone that sounded like some old sci-fi show. Jack chuckled at the music.

"Jack, can you please put the phone on vibrate?" said Grace.

"Sure, sorry hon, but don't you just love that new ringtone?" joked Jack as he turned the ringer to vibrate only.

She smiled, lifting her head off his shoulder, and replied, "Let me think about that for a minute…NO," and she leaned back and continued watching the kids on the street.

He glanced at the phone's screen and noticed that it was a text from Paul McGuire. Paul was one of Jack's closest friends and business strategist for years and had the unique ability to find money and talent under the most obscure rocks. He had partnered with him on multiple ventures over the years.

Paul's text simply read, "Hey Jack, what's up?"

Jack always had a very hard time relaxing and thought, *Now would be the perfect time to try out my latest prototype,* and he got up to go into the house.

"Jack, where are you going? We've only been out here for five minutes. Can't you just sit with me for a while?"

"Sure hon, I'll be right back. I just want to try something."

"It's Sunday. Please tell me it's not work-related."

"No, I just want to try something with Paul. He just texted me and I want to answer him using the Mindset."

Grace knew what he was up to and knew it was no use. Jack was going to do what he wanted.

As he entered his home lab in the basement, he looked like a child grinning with excitement. The lab was very neat and tidy. The far wall contained diagrams of the human brain, electronic circuits, logical workflows and database architectures. The other walls were covered with bookshelves containing hundreds of medical journals and electrical, chemical and mechanical engineering textbooks.

In the center of the room sat a raised workbench made out of thick wood illuminated by several hanging spotlights and one large movable light. Attached to the desk was a six-inch magnifying glass.

The desk was covered with a soldering iron, spools of different types of wire, various high-precision tools and a 3D model of the human brain. In the center of the desk was the head of a mannequin wearing what appeared to be a head harness constructed out of rubber straps and silver sensors. Wires attached to the sensors converged to a smartphone plug. Jack picked up the head harness and placed it over his head. He then inserted the plug into his smartphone and looked down at the screen.

Jack had put in months of late nights on his new tech but the previous night he had finally solved the last few bugs in the code. The Mindset was finally done.

"OK, here we go," he said to himself and pressed the switch on the wire leading into the phone. Instantly he felt a slight headache and grabbed his head.

What is that pain? It can't be the Mindset, he thought as the pain slowly subsided.

Now looking down at his smartphone, he entered the messaging app and without saying a word, 'Not much, you?' magically appeared on the screen, right below where his friend Paul had texted, 'Hey Jack what's up?' only a few minutes ago.

The head harness contained electro-encephalogram (EEG) sensors that picked up Jack's brainwaves and then sent the signals through the wire to his smartphone app, where his thoughts appeared as text on the screen. The Mindset learned by listening to his speech and typing patterns. It then matched the text to the corresponding brainwave and stored the relationship in the cloud. When Jack thought of something to text, the application would try to match his brainwave to previously recorded relationships. If the match was made, the app displayed the correct text inside any text field on the smartphone.

Jack giggled like a little kid and hit the arrow button on the phone to send the text. He then ran upstairs, still wearing the headgear.

"Grace look, I just sent Paul a text through the Mindset app without even saying word," he laughed and continued to grin in self-amusement.

"That's nice hon, but please don't let the neighbors see you like that. They already think you're crazy," she smiled, obviously still trying to relax.

"But it works! I stayed up late last night and I think I got all the bugs out of it. This is huge for us," said Jack.

"Good, now can you sit with me for awhile?" she asked nicely.

"Grace, you got to admit, nothing is more appealing than not having to type a single word on a little keyboard again, especially while driving," he bragged.

"I can think of many things more appealing, Jack," she said, still trying to relax.

"Come on, like what?"

"Like a relaxation machine?"

"Oh Grace."

"Seriously, can't you just sit with me for an hour and relax without being distracted by some form of technology or work?"

"I was relaxing Grace, but I just wanted to try the

new Mindset prototype with Paul. I have to go to the Mindset headquarters in LA this week and they're waiting for the final code for mass production," answered Jack. At that moment another text came in, making the same geeky sci-fi music tone.

"Jack, I thought you shut off that ringer," pleaded Grace.

"I did. Sorry, I must have hit it by accident," said Jack, as he looked down at the phone.

'You're thought-texting me, aren't you LOL?' wrote Paul.

Jack grinned again and looked down at the phone, and like magic, the words, 'You bet brother; this technology is absolutely amazing' appeared on the screen and again Jack pressed the arrow to send.

Intrigued, Paul quickly replied, 'I'm calling you now,' and Jack's smartphone rang in a longer, louder version of the same tune. Grace rolled her eyes while Jack got up quickly to take the call inside the house.

Before Paul could even get a word in edgewise Jack blurted, "The Mindset's software is done Paul; it really works seamlessly!"

"Wow, that's incredible! What's next? When are you back at Mindset HQ? I want to meet you there," asked Paul.

"Actually, I have a meeting with Charles this week to sign the MediaCAST licensing deal. I will be there on Thursday. Can you make it?" asked Jack.

"Definitely, I'll book the flight and I'll see you in LA in a couple of days. I'm really excited for you bro; this might be the big one you've been waiting for," replied Paul.

"I know. It doesn't seem real. I can't wait to see you, bud," said Jack.

"Definitely brother, you take care and I'll see you soon," replied Paul.

"You too, I'll see you at Mindset," and they both hung up the phone.

Jack continued to amuse himself by thinking of random words and phrases that quickly appeared and disappeared on the smartphone display. If the words or phrases Jack thought were not in the cloud, then nothing appeared on the screen. That would force Jack to say the message or type manually. As Jack spoke or typed new words or phrases, the Mindset would continue to learn. The longer Jack used the Mindset, the smarter it seemed to become, and sometimes it felt like it knew what Jack was thinking even before he did.

This thing is scary at times, he thought, smiling.

After playing with his devices for a while, Jack placed his hands on his temples. He was obviously still experiencing minor head pain. At that moment Grace walked in.

"Are you OK?" she asked, concerned. "Is that

device good for you, Jack?"

"Sure it is," answered Jack. "This is just a migraine; you know I get them every now and then. It's from straining my eyes."

"Really, I think you need to unplug, Jack," Grace said. "You seem to be getting more and more headaches every day."

Jack carefully pulled the Mindset off his head.

"OK, but it's not the Mindset, it's just too much time on the computer. Don't worry about me, Grace," said Jack, trying to minimize her concern.

"If you say so, hon," she replied, unconvinced, and went into the kitchen.

Chapter Two

Jack had run several companies over the last 20 years and had come to realize the title of CEO was overrated. So, he had partnered with another old friend, Charles Scuttles, to run the Mindset Corporation in Santa Monica.

The partnership with Charles had helped Jack to build a world-class team of neuroscientists, engineers, mobile app software developers, product designers, and marketing experts. The team had been focused on styling, micronizing, packaging, and branding the Mindset technology for the consumer smartphone industry, but they had been waiting for Jack to tweak the software algorithms before launching into production.

Jack had only seen a 3D rendering of the preproduction prototype model, so he was excited to get to the Mindset HQ and see the sleek new device that had Bluetooth, camera, headphones and microphone all built in.

It was 8:58AM when Jack drove into Mindset's new headquarters off Ocean Park Blvd. The parking lot was newly paved and lined with beautiful palm trees. The lot was already packed so he had to drive all the way around to the far side of the building to find a spot. As he navigated around the new building, the size and level of construction amazed him. Charles had mentioned they were building a new HQ, but this was unbelievable. It was a very large three-story, hi-tech, blue pentagonal glass structure with a glass-domed roof.

"I wonder where the money to fund this came from?" he said to himself. "Especially since the last location was a small warehouse in Van Nuys."

Finally he found a parking spot and climbed out of the rented black Mercedes 350. The temperature was far cooler than a usual LA morning.

I need my jacket, he thought as he grabbed it from the back seat and placed his larger than average sized wallet in the right inside pocket. He then grabbed his Mindset prototype and put it on.

I'll use the Mindset to send Charles a quick message to let him know I'm here, he thought, then locked the car and proceeded to the front door.

After walking through the rotating glass front doors, he entered into the main lobby, where he noticed a beautiful blond woman in her mid-twenties, wearing a white business dress and working at a new Apple computer. The sight of her made him completely forget he was still wearing his crude-looking Mindset prototype.

The reception counter was paperless, stainless and glass. Multiple LCD screens covered the entire wall behind her, making the wall appear as one display. Unique images of sea life flowed on and off the screen in a fluid motion. About every minute the wall would go completely white and the Mindset logo would appear directly in the middle. It was absolutely mesmerizing and gave the feeling that this company was in the elite of the elite.

The comparison of the old office to new office was hard for Jack to fathom.

How was this possible? he thought. *This building must have cost over $200 million.*

As he approached the counter, he placed his phone down, looking for the visitor sign-in book. His Mindset was still tethered to his phone.

"Please scan your driver's license into the digital visitor log, sir," she said and pointed to the computer screen that was embedded into the counter surface.

"Ah, sure," replied Jack, trying to act cool. He removed his wallet from his right inside pocket. Quickly, he scanned his driver's license over the screen, returned his wallet to his jacket pocket and then thought, *Man this company's got a lot of class. Look at this smoking hot receptionist; I wonder how much she's costing the company?*

Then he noticed the receptionist staring down at the screen of his phone. The phone display read, 'Man, this company's got a lot of class. Look at this smoking hot receptionist; I wonder how much she's costing the company?'

Startled he thought, *Oh crap,* and immediately 'Oh crap' appeared in the text field. The receptionist giggled. Jack grabbed the phone and started to fumble with the controls as though he'd never seen technology before in his life. Then he pulled the Mindset prototype off his head to kill any chance of more stupidity coming out of his brain.

Still smiling and in a professional manner, the receptionist said, "Welcome Mr. Cooper. You're here to see Charles. I've been waiting for you. By the way, Mr. McGuire is already here."

"Err, yes, yes, Charles Scuttles, that's right. I'm here to see Charles," he stuttered, obviously still very embarrassed.

She smiled and without making a call, she replied, "Charles is ready to see you now." Immediately, two parts of the LCD wall behind her pulled back and opened in a robotic and fluid fashion. The doors revealed a huge pentagonal atrium with about a hundred people wearing white lab coats, bustling about. This was definitely not the typical flip-flop startup company he remembered.

"This has obviously been funded by some serious venture capital money," he said to himself.

The atrium was absolutely beautiful, with palm trees and tropical plants intermingled with waterfalls and hi-tech sitting areas. The huge area was covered by the glass dome that Jack had noticed from the outside and surrounded by three stories of blue tinted glass offices with connecting escalators that moved the white-coated employees from floor to floor.

As Jack scanned over the atrium, he then noticed something not so beautiful and even unnerving. The room had armed guards in black uniforms at every exit and on every floor.

That's interesting, he thought to himself.

Charles' assistant Chris Tiller met Jack at the entrance to the atrium. Chris was about six foot, thirty years old, with a lean build, and short, slicked-back blond hair. Chris was dressed in a perfectly groomed black suit with some sort of expensive watch. He looked like a GQ model.

"Good morning Mr. Cooper, as always, nice to see you," said Chris in a clear, butler-like, fake English accent.

"Good to see you too, Chris. I see a lot has changed around here," replied Jack, still remembering when Chris wore flip-flops at the other location.

"Yes, Jack, things have changed a lot. Charles and Paul are waiting for you in his office. I will escort you," said Chris.

"Escort me? Can't you just tell me where to go?"

"Sorry, I can't do that Jack," said Chris.

"Why? What's with all the security? Seems a little

excessive for a technology company," questioned Jack.

"It's the new security protocols."

"Protocols? Are you serious?"

"I'm afraid so, Jack. We have to follow proper security procedures now that we are doing military contracts," Chris replied.

"Protocol--well, you even sound military. I didn't know you guys were even working on military tech," replied Jack.

Chris just smiled as they continued around the perimeter of the atrium, and then up the stainless escalators to a second level of glass offices. As they walked along the upper balcony overlooking the atrium, they passed several glass conference rooms and large work areas on the other side. More white-coat employees scurried around in the large work areas, while others worked on 3D CAD software and a variety of other software programming environments that Jack recognized.

The last work area before the elevator contained approximately ten testing centers, where Jack noticed men in military clothing. All of them were wearing newly redesigned preproduction versions of the Mindset. The device was now very compact and completely wireless. The styling was unique and, at first appearance, it looked like a thin pair of highly metallic glasses worn backwards. Jack remembered that the new product was made of high-strength carbon fiber titanium composite that was nearly unbreakable. The shape of the Mindset resembled the letter M on both sides of the arms that wrapped around the head, over the ears, and extended to the temple area. A blue light seemed to surround the head while the device was in operation and pulsed when communicating data.

That's very cool, almost angelic looking, he thought to himself.

The soldiers were directly interfacing with both testing engineers and scientists, and the process looked like something out of a science fiction movie.

Hmmm, why would the military be so interested in thought-to-text messaging technology? Jack thought.

Chris then guided Jack toward a stainless elevator door at one corner of the pentagonal building. As they got closer, he noticed two armed men in black uniforms guarding the elevator.

Without pushing a button, the elevator door opened and Chris guided Jack in. The elevator smelled new, even stronger than a new car.

As the doors closed, Jack realized the elevator had no buttons inside, and just as he had time to ask why, the door closed and the elevator automatically started moving. It seemed to move fast and was definitely going downward, which made no sense.

"I'm confused. Why walk up to the second floor to

go down, Chris?" Jack asked.

"Not too sure, Mr. Cooper. I didn't design this place; I just work here," he smiled.

After about 5 seconds, the doors opened to reveal a huge, beautiful sixty foot in diameter round office with LCD screens covering the entire wall in 360 degrees.

There was a ten-foot walkway all around the perimeter of the room, while the center was sunken about four feet and was close to forty feet in diameter. The sunken area contained several high-tech couches, tropical plants, and three large round tropical salt-water fish tanks. The ceiling was dome-shaped and made of blue tinted glass that seemed to give a view of the sky even though that was not possible because they were far underground.

Must be some form of lighted simulation or screen projection, Jack thought.

On the far side of room, and on top of the walkway, he noticed a single glass and stainless steel desk with a cool black nylon and stainless chair. The desk was spotless and contained no paper or mess.

Chris guided Jack down the steps to the sunken area, where Paul and Charles sat laughing and drinking what appeared to be wine.

"Early in the morning for alcohol, isn't it boys?" Jack smiled.

"Celebrations have no defined time, my brilliant

friend," replied Charles.

Charles Scuttles was fifty-five years old with gray hair, six foot with a slender build. Charles was a college tennis player in the day and still played occasionally to stay in shape. Paul was forty-eight years old, five foot ten inches and one hundred and seventy-five pounds with thinning hair and glasses. Paul never seemed to be serious and was always cracking jokes--in Jack's opinion, at the wrong time.

There were also two beautiful women dressed in white business dresses waiting in the wings to serve them. By the elevator two large armed guards dressed in black uniforms also stood by.

"What's with all the guards?" Jack asked.

"They knew you were coming," Paul joked.

"Funny," Jack replied, not impressed.

"Seriously, what's with all the security, and this amazing building--how did you fund it?"

Charles abruptly stopped smiling, stood up and replied, "Let's just say we have a new investor and a new military contract that believes your IP needs to be better secured and further expanded."

"Hold on, you said my IP--you must be joking. I didn't invent any military tech or authorize the licensing of such tech, Charles," Jack replied.

Paul and Charles looked at each other and smiled.

"Well, the cat's out of the bag, Buddy Boy. We just landed the largest military software contract in the history of the world," bragged Charles.

"How, when, what do you mean, 'we'?" Jack sputtered, obviously blind-sided.

"Jack, it's time to talk about the new direction of your tech. We all know your thought-to-text message app is neat, but neat is not going to maximize its revenue potential," sold Charles.

"Charles, the licensing revenue for smartphones is huge; you're the one who told me that. So what do you mean maximize, and when did you change your mind?"

"I know what I said, Buddy Boy, but think military advantage for a minute," Charles replied, still in sell mode.

"Military advantage--I'm confused. You've always told me to stay focused so I don't really know what we're talking about. I mean, what's going on with the smartphone licensing agreement with MediaCAST?"

MediaCAST was the largest telecommunication company in world and Charles had been negotiating the distribution deal to install the Mindset app on all their new smartphones.

"Well, there are a couple of glitches with the deal, but to make a long story short, they want too much."

"Glitches? OK Charles, what the hell is going on?" said Jack, obviously getting agitated with Charles' persistent lying.

"They backed out. They believe they have their own tech. It would just be an ugly court battle so we're just going to move on to bigger opportunities," Charles confessed sheepishly.

"Move on?" Jack raised his voice. "You told me it was a done deal, Charles."

"I know, I know, but don't worry, Buddy Boy. We landed a huge military contract that is going to make the MediaCAST license deal look like rounding error."

Jack had known Charles for twenty years and he knew when Charles was in sales mode, and it was usually when he kept calling him Buddy Boy.

"This is priceless. I come here to finalize licensing agreements and now you tell me you've sold my tech to our government, without my authority," Jack said sarcastically.

"Hear Charles out, Jack," interjected Paul.

Now clearly upset, Jack turned to Paul. "What, did you know about this too?"

Paul bowed his head.

"Sit down and let's think logically about this," said Charles, trying to put on the charm.

"Logically? I haven't heard one logical thing come out of your mouth since I arrived this morning, Charles," snapped Jack.

"What if our police knew exactly what a criminal was thinking? They could head off crimes, murders, even rapes. What if our government knew what the other leaders were thinking even before and during negotiations? We would have a major global advantage," said Charles.

"Do you know what you're saying? You are turning this into a potential weapon, not a communication tool," Jack said. "How can you hold people responsible for their thoughts, when it's their actions that make them guilty? Just because some government leader thinks about war doesn't mean he would do it. Besides, you would have to make the person wear the Mindset to teach the system and record the brainwaves based on his or her vocabulary. This won't work, Charles."

At that moment Jack thought, *These guys have lost their marbles.* Immediately the text, 'These guys have lost their marbles' appeared on the wall screens all around them.

"See Jack?" Charles pointed at the screen. "The technology has advanced way further than you ever imagined. What do you think I've had my development team working on over the last six months? No disrespect to you, but texting software wouldn't have brought in this level of funding, Jack."

"So what? You're displaying my thoughts from my cloud account. Not really rocket science by any stretch of the imagination, Charles," Jack replied.

"Really? But you're not wearing the Mindset right now, are you, Mr. Genius?" smirked Charles. Then Jack remembered that he had removed the Mindset prototype during the embarrassing moment back in the lobby and it was now hanging around his neck

"What? I don't understand, how is that possible?" asked Jack, perplexed.

"Let's just say we enhanced your tech a lot, Buddy Boy. The question is, are you still on the team?" asked Charles.

Stunned, Jack sat down on the couch to think. He then realized they knew his every thought.

Charles continued, "We can now place long-range EEG sensors all around a room and we can learn people's brain patterns by matching them to their speech patterns. It's just like your application works with the Mindset app, only on a much larger scale."

"For what purpose, Charles?" said Jack still not buying the value of this direction.

"We would be able to know everything being thought in a room. This is a game changer for global negotiations, probably even stop wars, Buddy Boy," said Charles proudly.

"How about start wars?" Jack replied and the room went quiet.

Charles started to smile and then laughed. "Come on, Buddy Boy, it's not that bad. You're taking it to the extreme. Think of all the good that could come out it."

"Charles, I want to know who changed the focus. Who the hell is funding this project now? I know the Mindset Corporation added a new VC over the last six months. So who are they?"

"Jack, you worry too much. It's just a firm out of Pittsburgh, nothing to get concerned about. I'll send you all the details. Besides, I know you and Grace are struggling financially, so please let me worry about the positioning. You'll get your big fat check and the technology will help the world become a more truthful place."

Jack was trying frantically not to think about anything that would allow Charles know his real thoughts.

"I just don't know, Charles, I really need some time to think about it. I'll get back to you tomorrow," Jack replied.

As Jack got up to leave, Charles gestured to Paul to follow him to the elevator, where the two guards stood at attention. Jack looked at the guards and thought, *What a waste of money.*

Immediately, 'What a waste of money' appeared on the screen all around the room and Charles shook his head and said, "You'll never change, Buddy Boy. Just think it over; besides, this one is going make you rich."

Paul, Jack and Chris then entered the elevator and

the doors closed. Jack stood silent, not really knowing if they were still reading his mind. When the elevator doors opened, Chris escorted them through the building and out to the front lobby.

As Paul and Jack crossed the parking lot towards their cars, Paul asked, "Jack, are you OK?"

"Yes, I'm good, bud. I want you to meet me at Ming's tonight at five o'clock, OK?" said Jack without any emotion.

Jack had known Paul for many years, and he could sense that he was keeping something from him. The question was what, and how much did he know?

"Sure brother, anything for you, you know that," Paul replied. "I'll be there. Are you sure everything is OK?"

"Yes, I'm sure. Don't worry about me. I'm going to be rich, remember, and it's always been about the money, right?" replied Jack sarcastically.

"Come on Jack. It's not that bad. I'll see you at Ming's at five o'clock."

They both climbed into their cars and pulled out of the Mindset Corporation parking lot.

Chapter Three

Close to five o'clock Jack arrived at Ming's and parked around back in one of the three spots available for employees only. He walked through the back door and right into the extremely cluttered but spotless kitchen. There was always a strong smell of ginger, fish and some sort of cleaner, like Pine Sol.

Jack had been traveling to Los Angeles for business for many years and Ming's had become one of his favorite places to eat and just hang out after a stressful day. He knew everyone that worked there and it had become his home away from home. The owner's name was Que and all his employees also seemed to love Jack.

When Que saw Jack he left the wok cooking over an open flame and ran to hug him. One of the other cooks grabbed the wok, right as it was about to go up in flames. Que looked back and laughed.

In broken Chinese English Que said, "Jack, Jack, it's been so long, where have you been?" He paused. "I bet making new gadgets. Ha, ha, ha, ha."

Jack smiled and said, "No my old friend, I'm just tying to slow down, tired of inventing more junk. I should have been a cook like you, less headaches."

"No, no, you an amazing scientist, not cook. Go sit, your friend already here waiting for you," replied Que.

"Make sure you come out and sit with us when the

kitchen slows down, Que."

"I will, I will," said Que.

Jack walked out of the kitchen and into the small dining area, where there were about 10 tables and a small old-style sushi bar. The small restaurant was full and fairly noisy, with a couple of people lined up at the front door.

In the far corner, he noticed Paul sitting alone waving. Jack then walked over to the booth and sat down.

"Make sure your phone is off, Paul," said Jack.

"Well, hello to you too, brother. Being a little paranoid, I see."

"No, I just want to have a conversation where I don't have to worry about someone else eavesdropping," said Jack as he recollected the incident with the receptionist earlier that day.

"So it's been quite the day so far, my old friend. I bet you didn't see that one coming," Paul snickered.

"No, I didn't," Jack replied. "I think I'm just getting too old for this start-up tech bull-crap, or maybe I'm just growing a conscience in my old age. So, what do you think?" he continued, trying to keep the conversation friendly.

"That's a big question. About what?" Paul replied.

"You know what I'm talking about--selling the tech

to our government," answered Jack, getting a little annoyed with Paul's avoidance.

"Well, it depends on what hat I'm wearing. With my investor hat on I say sell it to the highest bidder and let's all exit. However, knowing you for years, I know you won't go against your principles, especially if you believe it will negatively affect others," said Paul.

"Listen, you know I originally built this technology for fun. If I had known that stupid little idea of thinking a text could be turned into a military weapon, I…" said Jack, but Paul cut him off before he could finish.

"It's not really a weapon; it's more like espionage or spying, isn't it?" Paul replied. "I don't think it will kill people, right?"

"I guess not. It just seems creepy that the government wants to be able to read your mind," said Jack. "Especially if a person's guilt could then be based on their thoughts and not their actions."

"I think you've been watching too many movies. Don't you think you're blowing it a little out of proportion, Jack? Charles said none of that. We, I mean Mindset, are talking about reading people's thoughts, not blowing up the world; besides, how's it any different from wiretapping phone calls or intercepting emails? You've got to remember that Charles is one of the best chief executive officers and you know that; that's why you went to him in the first place."

"Paul, you said 'we'--what do you mean 'we'? The last time I checked, you had only a handful of shares in Mindset," asked Jack.

Paul was obviously now uncomfortable and slightly squirming on the old bench seat. Jack could tell that the cat was, again, out of the bag. "Well," Paul paused.

"Go on," said Jack, now getting a little impatient.

"You remember that investment company out of Pittsburgh that Charles mentioned? It's owned by Rob LaVie," confessed Paul.

"ROB LAVIE," shouted Jack, interrupting the other patrons in the restaurant. Que leaned out of the kitchen to see what was going on.

"Sorry Que," apologized Jack.

Rob LaVie, in Jack's mind, was one of lowest forms of VC (Venture Capital) scum to ever to crawl on the face of the earth. LaVie had had a successful pro football career and had now run investment funds in technology over the last 10 years. Jack had been involved with him on one other occasion where the technology IP was stolen, but LaVie still became mega-rich on the deal.

Now in a much lower tone, Jack asked, "Why the hell would Charles deal with him? He knows how I feel about LaVie."

Paul continued, "I ran into Rob at a convention last year in Toronto. We started shooting the shit and one thing led to another and they decided to fund several project incubators, including yours."

"So you facilitated this, not Charles," said Jack leaning over the table so he wouldn't have to yell.

"I suppose I did," Paul admitted.

"Paul, you're supposed to be my friend."

"Jack, I am your friend and that's why I did it. I know you and Grace need the money and Charles was not raising funds fast enough. He was just leading you along with the whole MediaCAST license deal," explained Paul.

"I can't believe what I'm hearing," said Jack.

"Rob really wanted to help. He said he felt bad about the previous venture and wanted to fix things up with you. Dude, they put in $500M."

"I guess I don't know what to say. You're either the smartest investment banker I have ever met, or you just screwed me on another LaVie deal. I just don't understand--why wouldn't you tell me?" Jack asked disappointedly.

"You would have never of gone for it; you're too damn proud. I know you guys need money; you're still paying for your daughter in college," said Paul.

"It's not always about the money, Paul. Sometimes ethics and principles come into play," replied Jack, but he knew they needed the money. The previous LaVie deal almost bankrupted them and they were struggling to get their daughter through school.

"Well it's water under the bridge. The funding is all set and one of Rob's other portfolio companies is the company that helped to develop the EEG room sensors and the notification system. That's how Charles was able to read your mind today. To be quite honest that's way cooler than your tech anyway."

"You're just full of compliments, Paul. I think I've had about enough of this for one day," said Jack and he got up to leave.

"Que, please put it on my tab," yelled Jack.

"Damn straight Jack, but I thought you wanted to sit and talk," replied Que.

"We will. I'll be back later, Que."

Then Paul stood up. "Come on Jack, it will all work out, trust me. I'll call you tomorrow. It's time you sat in with Rob and Charles. They need your help to finalize the military licensing," pleaded Paul.

"Why?" Jack yelled back. "You guys seem to do everything just fine without me." As he walked into the kitchen, he gave Que a man hug and exited out the back door.

"Damn it," Paul said to himself. "Why is he so stubborn?"

As Jack drove back to his hotel he couldn't believe his friends would sell out to a scumbag like LaVie. Jack had known Charles and Paul for years and they had collectively started many disruptive technologies in the medical sector. Most importantly, all of these startups were committed to creating lasting positive social change. Charles and Paul had never crossed him before, so all of this made no sense, especially since they had both warned Jack not to work with LaVie on the last project.

As Jack turned onto Western Ave. he noticed that a black SUV had been following him for quite some time.

Paul's right, I must be getting paranoid, he thought. *Why would anyone need to tail me?*

Curious to see if the SUV would follow, he turned onto the I-10 ramp and peered into the rearview mirror. At the instant he took his eyes off the road, he heard a squeal of tires and the twisting of metal, combined with the explosions of the airbag and the shattering of broken glass.

The impact was so strong it flipped his car over and sent it skidding down the ramp on its roof. The car eventually came to rest about sixty feet from the point of impact. Jack hung there for a moment, disoriented. Attempting to crawl out of the car, the pain became unbearable, and then all went dark.

Chapter Four

Jack slowly awoke to an undecorated, white, sterile hospital room. As he blinked his eyes, he focused on the tubes that were connected to both arms and the bed covers that were wrapped tightly around his body. He was completely alone and the lights were dim.

It must be night, he thought as he slowly pushed the bed sheets off his legs and tried to sit up on the edge of the bed. Quickly he realized he was too unstable to sit up and fell back on the bed, flipping over one of the IV stands. The noise was so loud it alerted the nurses and they immediately ran in to reposition Jack back in the bed.

"Sir, sir, please lie down," said the nurse, and he lay back down on the bed.

"Do you know your name, sir?" asked the first nurse.

"Of course I know my name…it's…" but nothing came out.

"Sir, you've suffered a severe concussion and have been in a coma for the last two days," said the second nurse.

Not really understanding what she was saying, Jack asked, "Nurse, I want to go home."

"Where's home, honey?" the first nurse asked.

"It's ah…" Nothing came out and he started to get frightened and frustrated. Then it turned into anger and he started to get up.

"Quick, get the orderlies," the first nurse cried out. Two men then rushed in to hold Jack down while another nurse injected something into his IV. Quickly, Jack relaxed.

Dr. Gamble was new to the floor and just happened to be walking by.

"Nurse, what's going on?" he asked.

"This man was dropped off outside ER two days ago almost buck-naked. He had no ID, a concussion, some lacerations and a couple of bruised ribs. He's been in a coma the entire time. He just woke up and went all crazy on us. Joan just gave him a sedative he was prescribed earlier."

"Did you speak to him?" asked the doctor.

"Yes, I asked him his name and he didn't know it. I think he just a homeless crazy," she replied.

Annoyed with her comment, he said, "He doesn't look like a homeless crazy to me, nurse. I think it's better that we get to the bottom of this before jumping to conclusions, especially now that he's out of the coma. I want him restrained, the room guarded, and I'll see about getting the police over here to find out who he is."

"Yes, Doctor," she replied.

The next day Jack awoke, this time with his wrists strapped to the bed. "NURSE," he screamed, prompting her to run in.

"Relax sir, it's OK; you're in good hands here," said the nurse.

"Then why I am restrained? Let me up, NOW," ordered Jack. He was terrified and had no idea who or where he was, or even why he was there.

"No sir, I can't do that. I've been instructed to bring the police here when you wake up," she answered.

"OK, fine, get them here, just let me up," Jack yelled. She left in a hurry and Jack could see her dial some number through the doorway on his right. After about an hour, Jack watched two men walk up to the desk. The nurse then escorted them into his room.

"Nurse, can you please leave?" one of the men asked.

"Err, sure," she replied and left reluctantly.

"And Nurse, please close the door," he added, and she complied.

The men were both wearing cheap suits and one had sunglasses sitting on top of his bald head.

"Peter," said the man on Jack's left. "I'm FBI Agent Johnson and this is Agent Kloven."

"You called me Peter--is that my name?" Jack asked.

"Yes sir, we believe your name is Peter Molloy. Do you remember being in a car accident?" asked Agent

Kloven.

"Not really," Jack replied, now holding his head and obviously in pain.

"The car you rented was found smashed up on the I-10 ramp off Western Ave. Looked like you'd been in an accident with another vehicle; however, no other car was found. By the looks of your car, you're very lucky to be alive. Do you remember getting to the hospital, or who brought you?" asked Agent Johnson.

"No, no, I remember nothing," Jack grabbed his temples again as the pain seemed to increase. He felt bandages all around his head, but most of the pain seemed to be coming from in front of his ears.

Agent Kloven pulled out what appeared to be a wallet and keys. He then proceeded to remove the driver's license, looking at the picture.

"Yep, it sure looks like him," said Kloven and then handed the license to Johnson.

"I agree, that's him all right," he replied and handed Jack the wallet and keys.

Jack just sat staring at the contents of the wallet and then asked, "Why is the FBI involved?"

But before they had time to answer, Dr. Gamble entered the room and two men quickly exited behind him. It was as though they had been caught.

"They seem to be in rush. Are they friends of yours?" said Dr. Gamble.

"No, that was the FBI," said Jack.

"The FBI? Are you sure?"

"Yes, they brought me my wallet and keys," said Jack.

"Really," said Dr. Gamble.

"Yes, they're right here. At least I now know who I am," said Jack.

"So how are you feeling?" he asked.

"I feel fine, Doc. I'm just trying to put together all the pieces."

"Before I can release you, you have to know who you are and where you live," said Dr. Gamble.

Jack had this uneasy feeling that the two men had not been honest with him. His thoughts seemed crystal clear, almost photographic. But for some reason he didn't believe his name was Peter Molloy.

"So what's your name and where do you live?" he asked.

"My license says my name is Peter Molloy, and I live at 2708 Earle St. Los Angeles," he recited.

"But you don't remember that?"

"Not really, but if I go home I probably will," said Jack.

"Hmmm, we certainly don't want to rush things. Let's get these tubes out of you and monitor you overnight. I'll have you reevaluated in the morning and see about getting your family here. How does that sound?" asked Dr. Gamble, not really convinced that Jack was better.

"That sounds good," Jack replied, but he knew the doctor had no intentions of letting him leave unless a family member or someone close signed his release.

As Dr. Gamble left the room he heard him say to the nurse, "First remove his IV, then I want the room guarded--no one in and no one out. Got it?"

"Yes Doctor," she said.

As Jack watched her remove his IV he thought, *Something is definitely strange about this hospital. First the FBI shows up, and now the doctor wants me guarded. I don't feel safe in here. I need to get home, tonight.*

Around 2:00AM Jack watched the nurse walk by on her rounds and could see the overweight guard nodding off at the doorway.

"It's time," he said to himself.

The lights were low in the hospital and it was very quiet except for the odd beeping of medical equipment.

The guard was now completely asleep.

Not much protection, he thought as he crept past the snoring man and quickly travelled down the hall. He then noticed a pair of Crocs sitting in an open closet. He reached in and put them on.

Nothing makes any sense. Why can I think so clearly but can't even remember my own name? he thought, and performed complicated multiplication in his head, harder than he'd ever tried before.

12*17 is 204, 17*18 is 306. Wow, this is amazing, he thought, as he continued down the hall.

Finally, he made it out the side door of the hospital and looked down at his open wallet, displaying the driver's license.

"2708 Earle St. Los Angeles," he read. "If that's home, then that's where I'm going."

The problem was Jack had no idea how to get there or even where he currently was.

"I need to get on a computer. I bet there's one back in admitting," he said to himself and returned into the hospital building. Quietly, he snuck back into what appeared to be the admitting area with several admission stalls. Noticing a computer on every counter, he crawled over the nearest stall, from where the patient usually sat, and landed directly in front of an older desktop computer. Like second nature, Jack started to type.

How do I know how to do this? he thought. He opened up Google maps and clicked on the 'my location' icon in the lower right hand corner of the screen and looked at the address.

Wow, I'm pretty smart, he thought, and then looked

over at the wall where the hospital address was printed boldly on a poster.

"1225 Wilshire Blvd Los Angeles, CA 90017," he read.

"I guess that would have been easier," he smirked. Jack turned back to the computer and searched for driving directions between the hospital address and the address located on the driver's license.

"Five miles--that's not too far, but I can't walk it. I need a car," he said to himself as he noticed a banner ad that read, 'Uber, better, faster, cheaper...than a taxi'. "Well that was convenient! But how am I going to create an account?"

Then he remembered that the wallet also contained credit cards and several business cards.

"Well, if I am Peter Molloy, then I'll use these," Jack said to himself as he proceeded to create an account.

He began by typing in the email address p.molloy@zeeteo.com from the business card.

"Hmm password, let's make it 'whatismyname'," he said to himself.

When he was finished, he turned off the computer screen and quietly climbed back over the counter. After looking both directions, he sneaked out the side door and waited in the bushes for the car to arrive.

About 20 minutes had gone by when a black sedan

pulled up under the canopy.

"That must be it," he thought. Cautiously he approached the vehicle, while still trying to stay low and out of sight. Then, the driver's window wound down and the driver called out, "Hello sir, did you call for a car?"

Reluctantly, Jack replied, "Err, yes I did."

The driver stepped out of the car, opened the rear door for him and Jack climbed into the vehicle.

"So, where do you want go, Doc?" the driver asked.

He thinks I'm a doctor, he thought, looking at his hospital pants.

"I want to go to 2708 Earle St., Los Angeles, California," Jack answered.

"I know the area well, I grew up just down the road from there. Have you lived there long, Doc?" the driver asked.

"Err, I am not sure. I mean yes, a while," Jack replied nervously.

"I'll have you there in a few," said the driver and he turned out of the hospital parking lot.

As they drove, Jack watched the streets go by; however, he had no recollection of where he was or where he was going. Despite this, his thinking was getting clearer, and more precise.

If I could just remember who I am, he thought, but

it was no use, he had absolutely no recollection.

Finally the car arrived at the address Jack had provided from the license. The house was a small, run-down, single level frame house with shabby siding, missing shingles and a detached garage. The driveway was a combination of crushed stone and dirt that made a loud crunching sound as the tires drove over top.

"There you go, Mr. Molloy," said the driver as Jack climbed out.

How did he know my name? he thought.

"Hey wait, wait, how do you know my name?" Jack yelled back.

Stuttering, the driver replied, "It was on the order, Doc," and he quickly pulled away.

Of course, it must have been, he thought. *I'm just getting paranoid.*

After the car was gone, the street was dark and quiet. Jack stood there for a minute, staring at the house. The air was cold and Jack could see his breath. As he slowly approached the front door, a severe headache dropped him to his knees. It was the same type of pain he remembered from back at the hospital.

It must be from the accident, he thought as he pulled himself back up. When he got to the door he looked at the key ring that Agent Johnson had given him. The ring only contained two keys. One was a Jeep key-fob, and the other looked like a house key.

This must be the house key, he thought. As he pushed the key into the lock, a black cat jumped up on the steps and brushed against his leg.

"Hello little buddy, are you lost too?" Jack asked, obviously not expecting an answer. The door easily swung open, revealing a small living room, a bedroom, and a kitchen at the back. An old couch sat against the far wall, with an old wood stove to the right.

Slowly Jack walked into the middle of the living room. He was met by the smell of mold and a slight hint of pot.

"Is that marijuana? I don't smoke pot, do I?" he asked himself.

The room was almost completely empty, and the décor made it clear that the place had been vacant for quite some time.

"This isn't my house," he said to himself. Nothing seemed familiar and he realized he was no closer to knowing who he was or where he was from.

Distraught, Jack dropped to his knees, almost in tears, and started to pray, "God, who am I?" Then he noticed headlights pulling into the driveway and the scared cat took off running.

"I bet it's the cops," he said to himself. "I'm so stupid. I should have stayed in the hospital."

But it wasn't a cop car; it looked like that same black SUV that was following him before the accident.

Why does that vehicle look so familiar? he wondered. Anxious, Jack slowly started to move toward the back of the house. As he opened the back door he noticed two figures running in the shadows, and he knew he was in trouble.

I definitely should have stayed in the hospital, he thought.

Suddenly the figures both came into focus at the screen door and a petrified Jack fell to his knees in a weakened state of panic.

"OK, I'll go back, I'll go back," Jack yelled.

"What the hell are you talking about?" one of the figures asked.

Jack suddenly recognized the voice and immediately looked up and asked, "Who is it? Do I know you?"

"Of course, Jack. It's OK, Buddy Boy. It's Charles," and then in a flash he remembered. It was Charles Scuttles, with Chris Tiller from the Mindset HQ standing at his side, and his name was Jack Cooper.

"Jack. My name is Jack," he said.

"Of course it is, but the bigger question is why on earth did you leave the hospital, Jack?" asked Charles. "It's not safe for you to be out."

"Why?" said Jack.

"We have been following you since you left Ming's.

Paul was worried after you left the dinner meeting pissed off, so he called me."

"You are in a lot of danger," said Charles.

"From who, and why does my ID say my name is Peter?" Jack replied, obviously very confused.

"It's LaVie; he is trying to kill you, but there's no time for explanations, Buddy Boy, we need to go," replied Charles.

Jack then grabbed his head again in severe pain, and Charles realized he was in bad shape.

"Chris, he's a lot worse than I thought. Let's get him back to Mindset and fix up this mess," Charles barked.

"Fix what mess?" asked Jack.

"Jack, listen, you need to come with us. Only Charles can help you now," Chris said, and he slowly approached him.

As Chris advanced, Jack kept moving backwards. He was still confused, scared and unsure whom to trust. They seemed to be telling the truth, but how could he tell?

"Why did the FBI at the hospital tell me my name was Peter Molloy? They even gave me my wallet, my license, even my keys to this house," said Jack.

At that moment Jack's head pain returned and he fell to his knees.

"OK Chris, enough is enough. Let's get him to Mindset. We' got a lot of work to do to fix this mess," said Charles.

Chris nodded and they both picked him up and took him out of the house and into the black SUV.

As they pulled out and started driving down the road, Jack noticed headlights and looked back at the house.

"Hey two cop cars are pulling into the driveway of my house." Right as he finished saying 'house' Chris leaned over and injected Jack with some type of drug.

"What are you doing?" Jack yelled in pain.

"Don't worry Jack, it will help get rid of your headache," Chris replied and Jack was out into what seemed like a wild dream of colors and soothing sounds.

Chapter Five

Jack woke to find himself reclined in a high-tech dentist-style chair. His eyes felt heavy and dry, like sand had been thrown in them. It made him squint repeatedly to try and create more moisture to regain focus.

As his eyes started to recover, he noticed that the décor of the room seemed a lot like the Mindset HQ. However, it was a part of the building he had never seen before. Feeling his head, he then realized that he was wearing some sort of untethered rubberized cap that was interwoven with copper wires. Next to Jack was a machine that looked like a vital signs monitor; however, it was much larger in size and complexity.

Jack lay there wondering what had happened, and then he noticed Charles and Chris far across the room, sitting on a white leather couch, deep in conversation.

"Guys," mumbled Jack.

"Look, he's up, Charles," said Chris.

"You really had us all worried there for awhile, Buddy Boy," said Charles.

"I did? Why's that?" Jack replied, still a little groggy.

"How do you feel, Jack? Here, you need to drink some water." Charles handed him a bottle.

"No, no, I'm fine. Why am I in this chair and why are my arms held down?" Jack replied.

"What do you remember Jack? Try to think," said Charles.

"I don't want to think; just undo my hands and let me up," said Jack angrily, trying to pull on the straps that held his arms to the chair.

"Calm down Jack, it's not what you think," said Charles.

"Think? What do you mean think? The last thing I remember was leaving the dinner meeting with Paul at Ming's…" said Jack, trying to remember.

"Go on," said Charles.

"I was pissed, some idiot was following me. I remember turning onto the I-10 ramp and then…"

At that moment Paul walked into the room with Rob LaVie at his side. They seemed very friendly and were laughing out loud.

Rob LaVie was always dressed to the nines. He wore a black Armani suit and for some reason never seemed to age. Jack always despised snakes, and LaVie's long frame seemed to slither when he walked. His complexion was pale, almost without pigment, and his nose and ears seem to be slightly larger than normal. He had a unique attractiveness that was also in some way villainous.

Jack couldn't believe his eyes, but it was true; Paul, Charles and Rob were actually working together.

"You bastards, you used me like a Guinea pig." Jack

struggled to get up.

LaVie, if I could just free my hands, he thought.

'LaVie, if I could just free my hands' instantaneously popped up on the large wall display behind them.

"And you'll do what, Jack?" said LaVie. "Besides, what the hell did I do?"

"Are you mad? Why would you try to kill me over a stupid investment deal? I know you're a crook, but a murderer?" Jack snapped back.

"What the hell is he talking about?" asked LaVie turning to face Charles.

"It seems he believes you tried to kill him, Rob," joked Charles, "which is interesting because I don't remember that being a part of the memory implant."

"What memory implant?" growled Jack angrily, while still trying to free his hands from the chair.

Now gleaming with excitement, LaVie continued, "Don't you worry Jack, I didn't try to kill you. All those thoughts were implanted directly into your Mindset cloud account: the accident, the meeting at Ming's, the coma, sneaking out of the hospital, even your exit location where Charles and Chris picked you up and brought you back to reality."

"Really? If that's true then why restrain me? Release me now," said Jack, acting calmer.

"You're restrained because you know how you are after coming out of one of these memory implant tests. Do you feel like yourself now?"

"Yes, I'm good. Please let me up." But he was lying; he still didn't believe them and a burning rage was beginning to build up inside of him.

Paul released the straps holding Jack's hands. As Jack sat up and rubbed his wrists, Paul tried to hand him what appeared to be his cellphone. Jack looked at Paul and then at LaVie.

"You son of a bitch." In his rage he grabbed LaVie by the throat and knocked the phone out of Paul's hand. Paul and Chris quickly tried to restrain Jack but Charles also had to help contain him.

"Jack, stop!" yelled Charles. "It's not what you think. Look at the date and time on your phone."

Not listening, Jack screamed, "LaVie, I bet you were in the car that hit me. I was in a coma for two days."

Now released from Jack, LaVie started fixing his suit. "Are you crazy? Get this lunatic away from me."

"Lunatic--I'll show you who's a lunatic," screamed Jack, and he attempted to lunge at LaVie over Charles and Chris.

Then Charles picked up Jack's phone and placed it directly in front of his face until he took notice and read the display at the top of the screen.

"Look Jack, it's only 12:03PM on September 29th, that's today's date. It's still the same day you arrived here at Mindset from Michigan. Only three hours have passed," pleaded Charles.

"So what?" said Jack, still unconvinced.

"Listen Jack, if you were in a car accident and a coma for two days, don't you think it's strange that your wife Grace didn't come to see you at the hospital or even call you?"

Still struggling against their hold, Jack yelled, "I don't understand. I was in the hospital, I was in a coma for two days and I lost my memory."

"Are you sure, Jack?" smiled LaVie.

"Your technology works, Buddy Boy. You haven't even left Mindset. You've been here all along," added Charles. "It seems the memory implants have messed up your reality. You even said this might happen but it would be temporary."

"What do you mean I said? Placing a single thought is one thing, Charles; changing a person's reality is another. I don't believe it; you guys are lying," snapped Jack now standing by himself, rubbing his wrists from where he had been restrained in the chair.

"Really? Then explain why you have only been gone three hours, and why is no one concerned that you're missing?" said LaVie.

"I'm not sure, how do I know the time on the phone

is correct? You could have easily changed it," said Jack.

"Really Jack, why would we do that? If you don't believe us then call Grace. Actually Jack, use your own phone to call her," Charles challenged.

"Fine, I will." Jack snatched the phone out of Paul's hand, opened the contact list and clicked on Grace's number.

One ring, two rings, three rings…"Hello," she said in her usual happy voice.

"Grace, is that you?" Jack asked.

"Well of course it's me, silly, who else would it be. You dialed me, didn't you? So how are the meetings going? Are they productive?" she asked.

Jack fell back into the chair, speechless and seemed to lose his train of thought. He knew he had been in an accident, and he also knew he had been in the hospital, but the time frame made no sense.

Grace would have definitely come looking for me at the hospital, especially if I was gone for days, he thought.

"Grace, what time is it?" Jack asked.

"Here? It's 3:05PM. Are you at lunch?" she asked.

"Lunch." Then he realized she was back east and he was now on Pacific Time.

"I mean, what is the date?" Jack asked again.

"Are you messing with me, Jack? September 29th," she answered. "Are you OK?"

Paul, Chris, Charles and LaVie now stood there staring at Jack, smiling and laughing like it was a big joke.

"I'll call you back in a bit, hon," said Jack into the phone.

"OK Jack, talk to you soon." She hung up.

Jack got up out of the chair and walked toward the group. He was still light-headed and had to take a seat on the couch.

"Alright, what the hell is going on?" he said, now in a calmer voice.

"Slow down, Buddy Boy, and try to remember. Your technology doesn't just read thoughts anymore; we implant them," Charles tried to explain.

"You did it, you actually built a memory implant machine," LaVie added excitedly.

Obviously still upset, and very confused, Jack said, "So why was I forced to be a Guinea pig?"

"You weren't forced; you've always insisted on being the test pilot, Buddy Boy. We told you not to; try to remember," added Charles, now starting to get worried that they had fried Jack's brain.

"Do you really think I would trick you, Jack? Come on, we have been friends forever," said Paul.

At that moment Charles played the video of the implant process on the wall screen. The video clearly showed Jack insisting on being the test pilot and obviously leading the group.

It was strange because Jack still remembered the argument with Paul at Ming's, and it seemed so real. He felt like he didn't even know, or trust, anyone anymore.

"They're telling the truth, Jack. I've been here the entire time," reinforced Chris.

Obviously exhausted, Jack sat down in one of the six chairs surrounding a round glass coffee table on the other side of the room. The others followed like sheep.

"You've been the leader all along. You call the shots, not us. Remember, it's your technology," said LaVie.

It was obvious that the memory implants had affected Jack's rational thinking. His mind did not seem to be as clear as he remembered from back in the vacant house. In this reality, everything seemed far more challenging, like the feeling of walking in sand.

Maybe this is the real world, but I don't like it, Jack thought.

'Maybe this is the real world, but I don't like it' appeared on the display on the wall and the entire group started to laugh.

"At least your wireless EEG cap still seems to be

working, Buddy Boy," teased Charles. Jack started to relax and cracked a small smile. Slowly his mind seemed to be recovering and everything around him seemed to become real.

Remembering his dream, Jack said, "I thought you figured out how to read brainwaves without the cap, Charles."

"We only wish, Jack. That tech is far beyond anything we can build right now."

"Well, if all those thoughts were implanted, then I am a genius," said Jack and they all started to laugh. Jack then undid the straps, removed the EEG cap from his head and rubbed his face.

"What a wild ride," said Jack, now in a much calmer mood. The group laughed and started to discuss places the technology could be used and how much revenue it could generate.

"Military training," said Charles.

"Vacation implants," LaVie added.

"Homeland security," said Chris, and the list went on.

Jack sat listening to the group but thinking, *Something isn't right. I would never support this type of technology. It's too powerful. It's not who I am--or is it?* But he was afraid to say anything wrong.

"Yes, yes, they're all good ideas. Sorry guys but I really need to get some rest," he said, now starting to remember that he was staying at the W Hotel.

"No prob, I'll take you back to the W. You need a good night's sleep to get your energy back. That must have been hard on the old bod, and you're no kid anymore," teased Paul.

"OK Paul, I'll take you up on that. I'm not much for driving right now."

"I bet," said Charles.

"I'll get to bed and we can get an early start here tomorrow," replied Jack. "Let's all meet back here at 9:00AM. Now that we know the tech works we just need to define the market and key buyers."

"Now you're talking, Buddy Boy, but I have to say you sure had us worried. I thought you weren't coming back."

"It will take more than a few memory implants to keep me down, Charles."

"Good, we'll see you tomorrow 9:00AM sharp," Charles replied.

Jack and Paul headed toward the door when Jack remembered that he had brought his jacket because it had been unusually cold that morning.

"Where's my jacket, Charles?" asked Jack.

"I don't remember you bringing one in, Buddy Boy, but I'll get Chris to check back in my office." Chris quickly left the room to look for Jack's jacket. The room went quiet for a minute while Chris was gone, and for some reason Rob looked uneasy. Jack's mind was slowly getting clearer and clearer since he removed the EEG cap. But all the implanted stories seemed to be in front of his real thoughts. It was like reading a book at the same time as recalling a vacation trip.

Finally Chris returned from Charles' office but with no jacket.

"I don't think you brought one in, Jack. It's definitely not in Charles' office," said Chris.

Jack tried hard to remember and thought, *if I started the day at Mindset then I know I had my jacket. I clearly remember the cooler that usual LA morning, grabbing my jacket, the beautiful blond, scanning my driver's license, placing my wallet in the right jacket pocket and of course the embarrassing moment. How could I ever forget that?*

"My jacket had my wallet and keys in it," Jack said, "so I'm not going anywhere without that."

"Oh, your wallet and keys are over here Jack," Charles yelled from across the room. "They were right next to the memory implant chair. You removed them from your pants pockets right before we started the test pilot."

Jack's wallet was larger than usual so he never kept it in his pocket because it just wouldn't fit. As a matter of fact, he was always leaving it around. Grace was always on him about losing it.

Then it hit him. *Why is Charles lying about the wallet? He knows I never keep my wallet in my pants. He razzes me about it more than Grace does.*

Charles tossed the wallet and keys to Jack and winked without LaVie seeing.

"Thanks. I guess you're right, Charles." Jack walked toward the door of the room, with Paul and Chris following behind.

"So I'll see you all back here tomorrow at 9:00AM," said Jack, still thinking about the wallet.

"Sure will, Buddy Boy," yelled Charles as Jack and the others started to exit the room.

Jack looked back and caught LaVie staring at Charles like he had done something wrong.

What are they up to? he thought.

Chapter Six

As Jack walked beside Paul they crossed the beautiful palm tree lined parking lot.

"What a déjà vu," he said to himself.

"What did you say?" asked Paul.

"Nothing, just talking to myself."

Jack then noticed that his rental car had been moved a couple of parking spots over.

"Paul, did someone move my car while I was out?" he asked.

"Of course not, why would we do that?" he asked.

"I guess they wouldn't. It seems my mind is still a little fuzzy from the test," said Jack.

"Leave your car here and I'll drive you back to the W Hotel, you're in no condition to drive."

"OK Paul, but let me see if I left my jacket in the car," he said and pressed the keyless remote to unlock the doors. There, to Jack's amazement, was the jacket sitting on the rear seat.

I'm positive I grabbed it this morning. There's no way the memory implants could have messed me up this bad, he thought.

Jack was very confused and climbed into Paul's new Chevy Corvette.

"Driving in style, I see," said Jack.

"It's an exotic rental. I thought I'd give it a try."

"Exotic? Corvette is American isn't it?"

"Yeah, well, you know what I mean. Just recline the seat and relax. You had a busy day," said Paul and he pulled out of the parking lot while Jack looked back at the car he had rented in the morning.

"A silver Mercedes 350?" he said to himself.

"You talking to yourself again?" teased Paul.

"Paul, wasn't my rental car black?" asked Jack.

"Not sure Jack, I was already at Mindset when you arrived, remember?" replied Paul nervously.

Jack knew the rental car was black and he also knew he had his jacket. Nothing seemed to make sense. Obviously he knew the memory implanting had messed with his sense of reality, so it was possible he was still feeling the side effects.

"Paul, just get me back to the hotel. I definitely need to rest," said Jack.

"That's the smartest thing you've said all day. I'll have you there in a jiffy, my old friend," replied Paul as he squealed the tires around the corner. After they had been driving for a while, Jack looked down and realized he was still holding onto the single-fold wallet Charles tossed to him. Slowly he opened it and to his astonishment the driver's license read 'Peter Molloy', with someone else's picture on it.

Jack froze in disbelief, and then looked down again. Obviously shaken up, Jack closed the wallet without showing Paul and tried to push it into his jacket pocket.

Why won't it go in? he thought. Then he realized that another wallet was already inside the pocket.

Am I losing my mind? he thought and rubbed his face. *Why would Charles have Peter Molloy's wallet when that was a memory implant? I wonder whose name and photo is in the other wallet?*

Now feeling very paranoid, Jack sat quietly, not knowing whom to trust. After a quiet and awkward drive, they arrived at the beautiful W Hotel in Westwood. Jack quickly exited the car and started toward the front door without saying a word.

"Hey wait, do you want me to walk you up?" asked Paul.

"No, I'm good. I'll see you in the morning," Jack replied, looking back.

He quickly entered the ultra-modern boutique style lobby and walked over to the stainless elevators, where he pushed the button and stood waiting. As the elevators door opened he thought, *What room am I in and where is my room key?*

Jack reached into the jacket and removed the other wallet. An Asian couple stood in the elevator waiting for him to press a button.

"What floor do you want?" the man asked, standing beside the buttons, ready to press it for him.

Awkwardly he removed his wallet from his jacket

to try and locate his room key. In one of the slots he saw a cardboard room key holder containing two keys. 701 was written in pen on the outside of the holder.

"Err, 7th floor please," he said, uncertain.

Afraid to look at the driver's license he pulled it out and read the words 'Jack Cooper', located directly beside his photo.

"Oh thank God," he said out loud as he quickly exited the elevator and walked down the hallway. The couple looked at each other and shook their heads.

"Too much partying," the man said to his wife and smiled, she nodded.

As he entered the room, he threw down the jacket on the chair and started to empty the contents of both wallets onto the king size bed.

"Why would Charles give me this wallet? If the accident and the hospital were a memory implant, then Peter Molloy and this wallet would not exist. What was Charles trying to tell me, or even warn me about?" he said to himself.

"What if this whole thing is just a setup by LaVie to prove me insane and steal the tech? I wouldn't put anything past him." Then Jack paused to think. "Yes, that's got to be it. I'm sure of it. Charles must be trying to warn me by giving me this wallet!"

Jack was now starting to think clearer again, just like he remembered back in the vacant house after the hospital.

"I need to go back to the hospital and the house to find out what's real." As that sentence left his lips he got another severe headache and collapsed on the floor. Like before, he experienced a mixture of wild colors and southing sounds.

After what seemed like seconds he awoke in a full sweat.

Where the hell am I, he thought to himself. He realized he was sitting up in his own bed back in Michigan, and the alarm was beeping and flashing 5:00AM.

Grace rolled over and whispered, "It's time to get up hon; you've got to make your LA flight"

"LA flight," he said.

"Yes, come on, get up or you're going to miss the 8:35AM departure. It's at least an hour's drive to Metro Airport, remember?" she said.

Wiping the sweat from his forehead he got up and turned on the shower in the en suite bathroom. Everything seemed like a blur; one memory bled into the next.

I wasn't drinking last night, was I, so why do I feel so hung over? he thought.

All the memories now seemed like dreams or even hallucinations.

"What is happening to me? Am I going insane?" he asked himself as he looked into the mirror.

"What hon?" Grace asked from the bedroom.

"Nothing, just talking to myself. I've got a busy day, you know," he answered as his voice cracked.

"I know, but you've been waiting and working so hard for this day. The MediaCAST license deal is so big, and you should be proud of yourself. I know Emma and I are very proud of you," said Grace as she walked into the bathroom.

Jack got out of the shower and dried off. He placed his towel around his waist and turned to hug and kiss her while she flossed her teeth.

"I know this is a big deal. I'm just trying to have the right mindset," he joked and they both smiled.

Chapter Seven

A few hours later, Jack sat on the plane in business class and started to recollect all the details of his dreams. He pulled out his tablet and put on his Mindset prototype. This Mindset looked more like the wireless pre-production version he remembered from the dream.

At least some things are the same, he thought to himself. He then began to recall the dreams. Quickly they appeared on the screen of his tablet:

- The new awesome high-tech Mindset building. Ocean Blvd in Santa Monica.

- Feeling the cooler than usual LA morning.

- Grabbing my jacket from the back seat of the black Mercedes 350 rental car.

- The beautiful receptionist sitting in front of the huge high-tech wall screen.

- The embarrassing moment in front of her with the thought-to-text app on the counter.

- Chris dressed like a GQ model.

- Walking through the new headquarters and seeing the pre-production version of the Mindset device.

- The argument about the military tech with Charles.

- The dinner at Ming's and the argument about Paul's alliance with the investor Rob LaVie.

- The black SUV following me.

- The car accident and how the impact and pain felt so real.
- Lying in the bed at LA Regional Hospital and seeing Dr. Gamble.
- FBI Agent Johnson and Agent Kloven calling me Peter Molloy and returning the wallet and keys.
- Sneaking out of the hospital and hacking a hospital computer and calling a cab.
- Calling a cab and going to the house address on the driver's license.
- Charles and Chris following me and meeting me at the house.
- Blacking out and being back at Mindset headquarters.
- The memory implants and control technology.
- Leading the implant testing pilot and voluntarily being the test subject.
- Paul partnering with, and trusting, Rob LaVie.
- Charles tossing me Peter Molloy's wallet.
- The different colored Mercedes 350 rental car.
- Finding the jacket and the other wallet.
- Blacking out at the W Hotel.

As he read back the list, he thought, *Wow, my technology really is cool.*

Jack wanted to add more to the list, but the memories were getting too overwhelming and he started to get another slight headache.

It all seemed too real, definitely not like a dream. I wonder if the Mindset device is responsible for these headaches and wild dreams. I've been using it a lot lately, he thought to himself, removing it from his head.

"No, the Mindset app only reads thoughts; it doesn't implant them. They must be dreams," he said under his breath, trying to convince himself.

"Did you say something, sir?" asked the old lady sitting beside him.

"Err, no, just talking to myself," he said.

"Those are very nice headphones."

"They're not really headphones. They are, but they're not," Jack stuttered.

"Whatever sonny. I'm sure you're not listening to any of that devil music," she smiled.

"Oh no, I wasn't listening to music. I was typing a message with my brain. You see, I invented this…" said Jack.

Slowly she leaned over. "You know, devil music is one thing, but you really should stay off the drugs, son." She patted his arm. Jack politely smiled back.

A few hours later they landed in LA. He grabbed his bags and walked out of the terminal.

I love palm trees, he thought.

His first stop was to get a rental car; so he crossed the road and headed toward the car rental shuttles, where luckily one was already waiting.

"Great timing, it's about time something went my way," he said to himself and climbed in.

Once at the rental place, he selected his usual pick, a red Dodge Challenger. As he climbed into the car, he looked at his watch and realized he had a bit of time before his meeting at the Mindset HQ in Van Nuys.

"I'll just drive by Ocean Blvd where the New Mindset building was located in my dream and that will put an end to all this craziness. The Mindset Corporation definitely does not have a new HQ!" he said to himself, and he drove off.

About thirty minutes later, he turned onto Ocean Blvd. Jack could already see an open lot where the high-tech pentagonal HQ had been located in his dream. The lot was lined with the exact same palm trees he remembered. As he drove closer, he noticed a huge pentagonal foundation under construction.

"What?!" he said to himself, stunned. Jack knew he had never been to this location before, except in the dream.

"How is this possible? Did I see the future?" he said out loud while driving slowly around the outside of the lot. Then he noticed a sign in front of where the construction vehicles were moving in and out. He let down the window and pulled onto the dirt so he was close enough to read the sign.

"The Future Site for The Mindset Corporation," he read out loud.

"Really." He kept reading, "A LaVie Holdings Investment."

"What? LaVie--I knew it, those bastards." He took a photo of the sign with his smartphone.

How would I know about the pentagonal building? Obviously it's not built, but it sure looks like it will be. How did I know the address, and LaVie Investments? he thought, now feeling anxious.

Very confused and annoyed, he headed for the 12:00PM meeting at the old Mindset HQ building in Van Nuys. As he pulled up he noticed that it was exactly how he remembered it: a typical startup, located in a small flex space building, with seven or eight cars out front.

As Jack walked in he immediately saw Chris seated at an old desk in front of the self-decorated entryway. Developers had formulas, cartoons and equations written all over the walls in Sharpie. Comic heroes and video game posters were also plastered all over the open areas of the cracked plaster walls.

"Now that's the Mindset I remember," he said to himself.

The room was fairly dark and contained a couple of old bench car seats used as couches. Chris was dressed very casually and was wearing his usual flip-flops. This was definitely not the slick dressed Chris he had remembered from the dream.

"Hi Chris," Jack said.

"Oh, hi Jack, how was the flight? Any bumps?" he said without the polished fake British accent.

"Good, good, no bumps. Is Charles in the back?" asked Jack.

"Yes, go right in. Paul's there too," he added.

Jack walked into the poorly lit work area that was about the size of two double garages. He quickly noticed the slight musty odor and three racks of old Linux servers, all flashing and humming, in the near corner of the room.

Against the far wall, four developers sat at workstations that each had three screens, all containing code. It was highly air conditioned and contained no windows, to keep out the hot California sun.

"Yes!" he said to himself and smiled confidently. "This is definitely the Mindset I remember."

As his eyes adjusted to the dim light, he saw Charles and Paul siting at an old round conference table in the middle of the room drinking a glass of wine and laughing and joking around. Two armed guards dressed in black uniforms stood at each exit.

As Jack walked up he said, "So what's the celebration, and what's with the armed guards?"

"They knew you were coming," Paul joked.

"Funny, Paul," Jack replied, not impressed. "More importantly, what the hell is this?" Jack held up the smartphone displaying the photo he took of the new Mindset HQ. He then zoomed into the part that read, 'A LaVie Holdings Investment', so they were both clear what he meant.

Charles abruptly stopped smiling and he replied, "Well, let just say that we have a new investor and a new distribution partner that believes your IP needs to be better secured and expanded."

"Hold on, you said a new distribution partner. Don't we already have one?" he asked.

Both Paul and Charles looked at each other and smiled proudly.

"Now you know Buddy Boy. We just landed the largest app distribution contract in the history of the world," bragged Charles.

"What? What do you mean we? When? How?" Jack sputtered, obviously blind-sided.

Charles continued, "Jack, it's time to talk about the best direction for your tech. We know you have issues with Rob LaVie, but..." Jack interrupted him.

"I have issues?! The guy's a crook, you know that," retaliated Jack, obviously getting annoyed with the direction that this conversation was taking.

"He's not that bad, Buddy Boy, and this time he

really stepped up to the plate. He's put in $500M; that's how we're funding the new HQ," replied Charles.

"At what cost, Charles? You didn't give him control, did you?" asked Jack. Charles then put his head down and Jack knew that he had caved.

"You've got to be kidding me. We have the MediaCAST deal. We don't need another investor or new HQ. And we especially should not be selling the farm to LaVie," Jack pleaded.

Charles' head was still down and Jack sensed something else was wrong.

"Well, there were a couple of glitches with the MediaCAST deal, but to make a long story short, it's not going to happen."

"Glitches, what glitches?" asked Jack.

"Well…"

"No BS Charles, it's time to level with me. What the hell is going?" said Jack.

"Well, they backed out. They think they have their own tech. It would just be an ugly court battle so we're just going to move on to other, bigger opportunities," Charles answered sheepishly.

"Move on?" Jack raised his voice. "You told me it was a done deal, Charles. That's why I flew in today, remember, to sign the license agreement!"

"I know, I know, but don't worry, Buddy Boy. We

got a better contract that is going to make the MediaCAST license deal look like a rounding error."

This definitely felt like déjà vu. It seemed just like the dream he had about the shiny new Mindset HQ, when they were all arguing about turning the technology into a military application.

"This is priceless. I came here to finalize licensing agreements and now you tell me that you've sold control of my tech to that scumbag LaVie without my knowledge or my consent," said Jack, starting to pace back and forth.

"Please, hear him out, Jack," interjected Paul.

Now clearly upset, Jack faced Paul. "What about you? Did you know about this too?" Paul bowed his head.

"Sit down and let's think logically about this," said Charles, trying to put on the charm, "Rob sits on the board of Xycom. They are MediaCAST's newest competitor, and LaVie got us the deal, Buddy Boy; you're already rich. Besides, did you know Rob plans to run for the US Presidency?"

"I don't care if he's next in line for the Pope. He's a scumbag and I want nothing to do with him. Do you understand?" said Jack.

At that moment Rob LaVie walked into the work area from the lobby, accompanied by two other men in black suits. As usual, Rob was dressed to the nines in his standard, very expensive, black Armani suit. Then, before giving any formal greeting, he said, "I can't wait for you to get out of this dump, Charles, and Jack, good to finally have you on payroll." He smirked with an obvious sense of self-satisfaction.

Jack's stomach turned over and he thought, *I'll never work for you*, and 'I'll never work for you' appeared on Jack's smartphone that he had left on the table. LaVie glanced at the text, grinned and then turned to Charles.

"Xycom just received the first production shipment of the Mindset devices, Charles. By the way, great job expediting the production in China; we at Xycom need every competitive advantage we can get."

"Not a problem, Rob," replied Charles.

"Xycom is also one of my main supporters for my run for the Presidency this year," LaVie added.

Jack tried not to choke at the thought of LaVie someday becoming the President of the United States.

"Well anyway, Jack, it's always good to see you. I know you're probably still pissed about the RenTech deal, but don't be. I'm here to make a truce."

LaVie slid him a wire transfer slip and an agreement across the table where Jack was now standing. He looked down at the slip and it read $25 million dollars, dated yesterday and wired directly to the bank account number of Jack's consulting company. Slowly he picked up the slip and stood there speechless and fell back into one of the chairs.

"Is this a joke? Can this really be real?" was all he was able to spit out.

"Oh it's real, and this is only the start, Buddy Boy," added Charles.

"All you have to do is sign the agreement and I'll authorize another $25 million to be wired tomorrow," said LaVie in his typical arrogant fashion.

"So we won't be doing any military applications or memory implanting schemes then, right?" he asked and tried to crack a smile.

"What on earth are you talking about?" replied LaVie. "Your tech is about to go on all of the new Xycom phones worldwide. We are supposed to surpass MediaCAST smartphone sales by the end of this year."

"Can this really be happening?" said Jack, bewildered.

How can LaVie be my saving grace, he thought.

"Yes Jack, it's really happening," said Paul, and LaVie, Charles and Paul all started laughing.

Jack removed the Mindset from around his neck and then thought, *I just can't believe it,* and sat waiting for another blackout to come, but it didn't.

This must be reality, he thought.

"As I said, Jack, it's good to have you on my

payroll. Xycom is going to want to advance this technology, so be prepared to make a lot more money," LaVie added as he moved toward the exit.

"We are having a launch party at Xycom tomorrow night in San Francisco. I want all of you to be there with your wives," said Rob as he exited the door and left with his same rude and demanding demeanor.

"Charles, have you and Paul had lunch? There's something I wanted to talk to you about, but I don't want to do it here," said Jack.

"No we haven't. Let's go get a bite," said Charles. "It's on me." They all exited out the front door.

"I see you've gone American. It's about time after driving those Mercs for all those years," said Paul as he noticed the red Dodge Challenger.

"Yeah, it's pretty cool. I'll follow you guys," replied Jack and he got into the car. Then he thought, *Mercs? When do I rent Mercs?* Then Jack had a flashback to the dream when Paul drove him out of the new Mindset parking lot. He remembered clearly the entire conversation about the Mercedes 350, and especially the fact it wasn't black.

"But that wasn't real; it was a dream, right? " he said to himself and squealed the Challenger out of the parking lot and down the street.

Chapter Eight

As they arrived at their favorite local Jewish deli, Jack searched for enough change to put in the meter. Paul walked over and handed Jack a handful of coins.

"Here, I always have these with me when I'm in LA," said Paul.

"Paul, what made you think I rent Mercs?" asked Jack.

"Well, don't you?" Paul replied.

"I don't think so," Jack replied, but he was not completely sure. In reality, the harder he tried to remember the types of cars he rented, the harder it became to remember.

As they entered the deli, they approached a friendly girl at the front.

"Hello," she said in what sounded like a New York accent. "Would you like a table or booth?"

"Booth would be fine," said Charles.

She then grabbed three menus and started to walk toward a booth closer to the back of the room.

"How is this?" she asked.

"Perfect," replied Jack and she proceeded to hand them menus and take their drink order.

After she left, Charles asked, "So Jack, what's on your mind?"

"Guys, I have been having some wild dreams and hallucinations; they seem almost real," confessed Jack.

"I hope they have beautiful women in them," interjected Paul, and then laughed out loud.

"Seriously Paul, I am concerned it might be the Mindset. I want to do more subject testing before we deploy it to Xycom. We need to make sure it doesn't negatively affect the users," said Jack.

"Unfortunately, that would be impossible. The pre-production prototype went to China a month ago. The first production shipment has already arrived from Xycom. They're already putting them in the stores as we speak," explained Charles.

"Already? That's too quick. I'm really concerned. We don't want to hurt anyone. Think about the lawsuits," said Jack.

Charles started to smile and then laugh. "Come on, Buddy Boy, you're taking it to the extreme. You've been under a lot of stress for a very long time. There's nothing wrong with you and besides, money is what cures all ills, my friend."

"The money will definitely take a load off my mind, I just don't want to blow it because we cut corners," said Jack.

"Jack, you're still using the initial prototype; you know the production prototype fixed a lot of the bugs," said Charles,

"Yes, that's true," agreed Jack.

"Good, then I think what you really need is a

vacation, Buddy Boy. Why don't you take Grace down to San Diego for a month and relax? I know you both love it there. You need to get out of Michigan for awhile," Charles suggested.

"You might be right, Charles, it's been a long time since I just relaxed and did nothing," agreed Jack.

"Now you're talking, Buddy Boy. We've got your back here at the HQ. It's just a waiting game now, until the Mindset devices are available for resale. The app software is already in both app stores and ready to deploy. Besides, I'm focusing on the new building right now so I don't really need an over the hill neuroscientist sitting around twiddling his thumbs," teased Charles.

At that moment the waitress approached the table to take their orders.

"What would you like, fellas?" she said.

"I'll have a Turkey Rueben and coffee, black," said Jack.

"What about you, honey," she said as she turned toward Charles.

"Let's keep it simple and give me the same," he replied.

"…and you?" she asked, looking at Paul.

"I'll have the lunch special."

"You got it, fellas." She took off toward the kitchen.

"I know you like this place, Paul, but we really should have gone to Ming's. We haven't seen Que for quite awhile," said Jack.

"Who?" asked Paul.

"You know, Que, the owner of Ming's, my buddy," replied Jack.

"Sorry Jack, but I've never heard of Que or Ming's; you've never taken me there," answered Paul.

Jack sat there for a moment thinking about the day he had argued with Paul at Ming's.

"Paul, what are you talking about? You…" Jack started to say but he stopped. *Is Ming's even real?* he thought. *It has to be; I have known Que for years and I know the address. It must be real. I remember; it's off Western Ave. on the border of Korea Town.*

Frustrated Jack got up from the table and threw down a fifty-dollar bill.

"Guys, I just remembered, I've got another meeting. I gotta go. Sorry, lunch is on me," said Jack.

"Wait, where are you going? You haven't even eaten." yelled Paul as Jack exited quickly out the front door.

"He's really becoming one strange dude, Paul. We're lucky to have landed this deal with LaVie before he went off the deep end," said Charles.

"Ain't that the truth, Charles; I'm definitely worried

about that boy," replied Paul.

Chapter Nine

About forty-five minutes later, Jack arrived at Ming's and, as usual, parked around back in one of the three spots available for employees only. He walked through the back door and right into the extremely cluttered but sterile kitchen. There was the same strong smell of ginger, fish and some sort of cleaner, like Pine Sol, he remembered from before.

As soon as Que saw Jack he left the wok cooking over an open flame and ran to hug him. One of the other cooks grabbed the wok as it was about to burst into flames. Que looked back and laughed.

"Jack, Jack, it's been so long, where have you been?" Que paused. "I bet making new gadgets. Ha, ha, ha, ha."

Jack smiled, "No Que, my old friend, just tying to slow down, tired of inventing more junk. I should have been a cook like you, less headaches."

"No, no, I told you before, you an amazing scientist, not cook. Go sit, eat. I'll join you in minute," replied Que.

"I'm not really here to eat, but I do want to talk to you."

"OK, OK, just give me minute," replied Que.

Jack walked out of the kitchen and into a small dining area, where stood the 10 tables and the small old-style sushi bar. As usual the small restaurant was almost full and fairly noisy, but no lineup at the front door.

Noticing a couple of seats open at the sushi bar, he yelled, "Que, I'll just sit at the sushi counter."

"Okay, Jack but why only eat sushi when Chinese is better," he said and laughed from the kitchen.

As Jack looked around the room he thought, *Well, at least some things don't change!*

Finally, things were beginning to feel normal when Que came from the kitchen, grabbed the chair beside him, turned it around and sat on it backwards, facing Jack from his right side.

"So, how you been, it's been, what, a month?" Que asked in his broken English, smiling from ear to ear. He reminded Jack of an old Jerry Lewis skit. He always made him laugh and feel at home.

"Yeah, I've been working on the next tech and it's, well, really consuming me," Jack replied.

"Sometimes you have to let your mind rest, Jack; not good to think all the time," Que said, "Remember what Asian proverb say: ***Tension is who you think you should be. Relaxation is who you are.***"

"You are very wise, my old friend; that's a good one, especially with what's been going on."

"I have time, you tell me everything. I let my wife handle kitchen and burn water, ha, ha, ha," said Que as he gestured to his scowling wife back in the kitchen.

"You're too funny, Que, you always make me laugh," said Jack.

"What been going on?" asked Que.

"So, I've been having these weird dreams or hallucinations. I see and remember places, people and situations that seem real but in many cases aren't," said Jack.

"Do these dreams have good or bad endings?" Que asked.

"Why would that matter?" Jack replied.

"The ancient Chinese philosopher Duke of Zhou created first Chinese dream dictionary. It became known as the god of dreams and he divided dreams in categories like the planets, weather, gods, spirits, the body and even disharmony," explained Que. "He believed that all dreams had significance."

"How does that apply to me?" asked Jack.

"O, come on, Jack, you smart guy. When your life is in disharmony your mind is also in disharmony," said Que. "I have known you for, what, 20 years? You're always worrying about something or building something. There is no real rest."

"Yeah, you're right Que, maybe I need to just let it go and not worry about these dreams anymore," said Jack.

"That's right Jack, forget them. It's just like I said to Paul the night you left in a huff, remember?" said

Que.

"What did you say?" Jack said, remembering specifically what Paul had said earlier about never being at Ming's, or knowing Que.

"You know, Paul, your friend," replied Que.

"Yes, yes, Que, I know Paul; when was that?"

"It was about a month ago, you remember; you were hot about something and you put the bill on your account."

Que got up and grabbed on old account ledger. "See I wrote it down: you owe me $24.33…plus tip, ha, ha, ha."

"Que, I don't understand. Paul clearly told me today he'd never been here before."

"Then I would say he's lying to you, Jack. He was very concerned about you, and you were in such a rush you also forgot your jacket," said Que. "Paul grabbed it and said he would give it to you. Actually, I think he said it even had your wallet in it."

Jack flashed back to the last time he remembered seeing his jacket in the back of the silver Mercedes 350 rental car and then laying it on the chair at the W hotel. This thought gave him a tremendous headache and he grabbed his head. But this time he did not black out. This was real and the pain seemed worse than ever before. He remembered that he was still wearing the Mindset and pulled it off his head and put it down on the counter. The headache went away immediately.

"It is the Mindset," he said to Que. "They are messing with my thoughts."

"I would say it's time to stop using it," said Que.

"It's not that easy; we sold them to Xycom, and the app is about to go onto every new smartphone," said Jack.

"Well, my friend, I am sorry to say, but you have big decision. Just remember other Chinese proverb: *A wise man makes his own decisions, but an ignorant man follows public opinion*," added Que. "So are you going to eat? It's on me, Jack."

"Sure Que, and thanks for the advice; you're the best," said Jack.

Que got up and went into the kitchen where Jack could hear him and his wife yelling back and forth in Chinese. For that one moment everything felt real. But he knew his life was about to get a lot more complicated. He had taken the money for a defective product that was about to go global.

Chapter Ten

The next day, Jack took a late flight from LAX and arrived in San Francisco around 7:00PM. Having been born in Michigan, Jack always enjoyed the San Francisco climate better than LA; however, he hated the thought of being in an earthquake.

Paul and Charles had arrived earlier and met him at the San Francisco International Airport. Jack threw his bag in the trunk of the Audi A6, hung his tuxedo bag in the back seat, and then got in.

Without even saying hello, Paul started on him. "I still don't know why you didn't take the early flight; then we wouldn't be late and you could have gotten ready with Grace at the hotel."

"What's the matter, you get up on the wrong side of the planet?" asked Jack, and then he thought, *What is with him? I'm the one that should be pissed at the liar.*

Jack stayed quiet, thinking of a tactful way to ask him why he lied about Ming's.

"So liar, why did you BS about Ming's?" said Jack in the most non-tactful and direct manner possible.

"Ming's? When did I lie about Ming's? Are you doing your crazy talk again? If so, please save it for someone with more patience," said Paul, not in his usual joking mood.

"I want to know the truth, Paul." Jack grabbed Paul by the shoulder from the back seat.

Paul pulled away and yelled, "Let me go, you nut; what's wrong with you? I told you I've never been to Ming's. Why would I lie about a stupid restaurant?"

"I wasn't sure why you would, Paul. So I went back to Ming's after our last lunch. Que said you were at Ming's with me last month and you even grabbed my jacket," accused Jack.

"Listen smart guy, I never went to LA last month. You went alone, remember."

Obviously confused, Jack still seemed to remember the meeting at Ming's as if it was yesterday.

"Listen, if it will make you feel better Jack, I'll go to Ming's with you and meet Que; then you'll know it wasn't me," Paul reinforced.

"OK, deal. As soon as we get back to LA tomorrow, we're going to Ming's," demanded Jack and then he leaned back in the rear seat and sat silently.

"Anything for you, bud," and Paul rolled his eyes as he looked over at Charles in the driver's seat.

"I must say you two are priceless today. A real joy to be around, considering you both just became multi-millionaires," said Charles as he shook his head and kept driving.

After about ten minutes of awkward silence they pulled up to the security booth of the underground garage of the Xycom headquarters. The building was about sixty stories high and was one of the tallest and most beautiful buildings in San Francisco. The underground garage was white and nearly spotless. Even the garage ramp was highly epoxy coated. The car's tires squealed while they descended around and around, deep into the ground.

"I wondered how these buildings handle the earthquakes?" Jack asked.

"Stop worrying about everything, Jack; this is supposed to be a party, remember? A good time, besides, our girls are probably already up there having a few drinks without us," Charles smiled.

"Not my Grace, she's not a drinker," Jack replied.

The posh valet attendant took the keys from Charles and opened the rear door of the Audi to help Jack remove his tuxedo from the back seat. Then they made their way towards the underground entrance. Jack soon noticed that they had to pass through what seemed like an x-ray machine that was manned by two security guards. *More security. And they think I worry about everything?* he thought.

"Please place all items on the conveyor and walk right through," the guard said sternly.

Jack placed his garment and shoe bag on the conveyor and walked through the x-ray machine like one would in an airport. A third guard sat at a desk directly in front of the elevators.

"Hello gentlemen, you must be here for the launch

party. Can I see all of your IDs?" the guard asked. They all removed their driver's licenses and handed them to the guard. The guard scanned their licenses and then handed them back with a name card that had their photo printed on it.

"Please wear this at all times while in the building," he said in a no-nonsense manner. He then hit a control behind the desk and the elevator doors opened.

"Enjoy your evening, gentlemen," said the guard, and they entered the elevator.

In what seemed like only a few seconds, they reached the sixtieth floor and exited into an elevator lobby. On the left they could hear people laughing and loud music playing through a set of double-tinted glass doors.

Two beautiful women stood at the doors and immediately moved toward them.

"Welcome, you must be Jack, Charles and Paul. It's very nice to meet you," one said. "I am Monique, Mr. McConnell's assistant, and I am here to help you in any way I can."

Mr. McConnell, aka "Mac", was the CEO of Xycom and a self-professed technology legend. Jack didn't care much for self-professed experts. He knew that the only thing Mac knew about technology was how to buy and sell things he didn't invent. However, Charles and Paul had always wanted to rub elbows with him.

"Monique, I still need to change into my tuxedo and shoes," said Jack, holding up the garment and shoe bags.

"We're sorry; he had a late flight," said Paul, obviously embarrassed as he apologized for Jack.

"It's quite alright sir, you can use Mr. McConnell's office to change. You're already somewhat of a celebrity here anyway, Mr. Cooper," she said. "Please follow me; his office is not too far away."

Paul and Charles followed the other woman and walked through the double doors into the party. Jack followed Monique to the right, in the direction of McConnell's office.

The hallway contained beautiful window offices on the left side and just a wall with Art Nouveau paintings on the right. At the end of the hallway was a set of double oak doors with the letters MAC engraved in gold on the doorplate.

Well, that's tacky, Jack thought. Monique scanned her ID on a wall pad and the door automatically swung inward, revealing a huge office overlooking the San Francisco harbor. The view was breathtaking.

"Wow, that's quite a view," said Jack.

"Yes, it is, isn't it? I never get tired of it," she replied in her seductive voice.

I bet you're in here with him all the time, he thought.

"The bathroom is on the right, Mr. Cooper. I will wait for you here," said Monique. Jack entered the bathroom and changed into his tuxedo. When he returned into the office, Monique was sitting on the couch with her legs crossed.

"You definitely clean up nice, Mr. Cooper. You're a very handsome man," she purred.

Not really knowing how to take that type of a compliment from a beautiful young woman, he replied, "Err, thank you."

"I will take you back to the party, Mr. Cooper, please follow me," she said. As Jack followed her toward the door of the office, he noticed an old college varsity football picture on the wall. In the picture was Mac, obviously from a much earlier time, standing beside another football player and holding a championship trophy.

That looks a lot like a young Rob LaVie, Jack thought.

"Monique, wait. What is the photo?" he asked.

"That's when Mac led Stratham to their first Division II football championship. Why do you ask?" she said.

"Well, the other person looks a lot like Rob LaVie," he replied.

She chuckled, "That's because it is, Jack. That's right before LaVie went pro."

"I didn't they know they went that far back,"

"Oh yes, Mr. Cooper. They've been friends for many years."

"Why didn't Mac go pro?"

"Not really sure, but I know they didn't win again after Mr. LaVie left that year, so that might be why," she said.

Jack nodded and they started to walk down the hallway to where the party was roaring along. As they entered through the double doors Jack was taken aback by the size of the banquet room and especially by the glass windows on the far side overlooking the city. The ceiling was two stories high so the room was obviously built using two floors, making the glass windows on the far side look like the sky.

As more people arrived into the room, five beautiful women handed out cool new Mindsets.

"Those must be the new production units Charles was talking about," he said to himself.

The women were working quickly to help everyone download the app and sync it with their smartphone via Bluetooth.

Black cocktail tables were spread throughout the room and were surrounded by groups of people in conversation. Everyone was wearing the Mindset and the blue light illuminated their heads like a halo.

"It looks so alien," he laughed to himself, "but cool

though."

"Here you are, sir," one of the women said.

"No thanks, I already have one," said Jack.

"Really, where did you get it from? These are all new," she said.

"I know the inventor," Jack replied and kept on walking.

The carpet was blood red with the Xycom and Mindset logos embedded into the design. On the right side of the room was the stage that had been set up with a large wall screen that reminded him of the wall screens he dreamt about at the new Mindset building. On the screen was a cool twisting animation that morphed into the Xycom logo and then the Mindset app logo and then finally faded, beginning the loop again.

He noticed his wife Grace standing at one of the front tables with Charles, Paul and their wives. Like everyone else, they also were wearing the latest Mindset.

Grace wore a black cocktail dress with sparkles and she looked exceptionally beautiful. He couldn't wait to hold her.

As Charles moved to the side he then noticed Grace drinking from a martini glass and talking to a tall, slender man in a black suit.

"That's funny, Grace drinking--very unusual," he said to himself.

As he got closer, the man slowly turned around as if he knew Jack was there.

"It's about time, Jack; you really shouldn't leave your lovely bride alone for so long. Some handsome knight might swoop her up," taunted LaVie.

"Then I guess it's a good thing there aren't any worthy knights around here, then," replied Jack sarcastically.

Grace looked at Jack and gave him the 'be nice' stare.

"I'm just joking, Rob; it's good to see you too," he added with little sincerity.

"What about me?" Grace asked. Then Jack realized LaVie had intentionally taken him right out of the moment and he had forgotten to even say hello or kiss and hug Grace.

"I am so sorry, Grace. You look absolutely wonderful. I really missed you over the last couple days. Was your flight from Detroit smooth?" he said and then tried to kiss her. Obviously she was still annoyed and turned her head, and Jack kissed her on the cheek. LaVie stared at Jack gleaming with pride.

"When am I going to stop letting LaVie get under my skin?" said Jack under his breath.

"What did you say, Jack?" Grace asked.

"Err, nothing, Grace, I said nothing," answered Jack, now also annoyed because she wouldn't give him a real kiss.

"Anyway, Buddy Boy, this is your party. You're the visionary around the tech; without you we wouldn't be here," said Charles.

"Yes, really Jack, you should be proud," added Paul.

"We are all proud of you Jack, but thanks to Rob we've finally got money in the bank," said Grace as she reached out and briefly touched Rob on the hand. Jack couldn't believe what he was seeing. He had never seen Grace drink alcohol, flirt with men, talk about money, and especially wear technology.

"There would be no money, Grace, without the product, and since when did you care about money?" asked Jack pointedly.

At that moment the waiters brought trays full of champagne glasses and bottles of Pernod Ricard Perrier Jouet Champaign.

That's around $50,000 per bottle, Jack thought. The lights started to dim and the windows seemed to magically become solid, thus no longer letting any light penetrate. Modern dance music started to pulsate through the air while laser beams and white lights danced around the stage and other parts of the large banquet room. Suddenly, a main spotlight appeared on the stage and Monique stood there alone in front of the video screen that projected her enlarged image. The crowd stood mesmerized, with their full attention on her beauty.

"Welcome everyone. It is my great honor and privilege to introduce the CEO and President of Xycom. Can you please put your hands together for Mr. Matthew McConnell," she said.

The crowd roared with approval as McConnell took the stage in a cloud of smoke, lights and music.

"Looks like the entrance to a football game, not a technology launch," Jack said to Grace.

"Be nice, Jack," Grace replied.

McConnell looked close to six feet and was slightly overweight. His accent sounded Texan but it was hard for Jack to be sure.

"Thank you, thank you…thank you, all of you," said McConnell over the loudspeaker system, and the crowd started to settle down to listen.

"First I want to welcome all of you to Xycom. You are about to witness the launch of the biggest game-changing technology since the invention of the micro-chip, and here to launch this new product is the brains behind this invention," said McConnell.

"I didn't know you were speaking," Paul whispered to Jack.

"I'm not," Jack replied.

McConnell continued, "Many of you probably

don't know this, but I played a little football in my college days. During that time I met a young man who had talent, charisma and vision. We were even fortunate enough to win the Division II championship together, which spring-boarded his career to become one of the greatest pro tight ends in the history of the game."

"He's obviously not talking about you, Buddy Boy," said Charles.

"Hmmm, you think?" Jack replied sarcastically, already realizing that Mac was talking about LaVie.

"But today is not about sports. I have watched this man grow in business and have come to respect his foresight. But his skills are now shining in the development and incubation of new ideas and technology," said Mac.

"I think I'm going to puke," Jack whispered into Grace's ear, and she looked back in slight disappointment at Jack's comment.

McConnell continued, "I believe this man is one of the brightest minds on the planet today, and he is the one who brought this revolutionary, one of a kind technology to Xycom. He is a new age genius and should be complimented on the Mindset application, the first thought-to-text technology. So please give a big round of applause to the brains behind the Mindset technology, Mr. Rob LaVie." The crowd roared again with applause.

Jack was so angry his hand started to shake and he accidentally spilled one of drinks on the table, thus knocking over a couple more onto Grace and Charles' wife. Rob LaVie, now on center stage, tried to start speaking but the crowd kept up the applause.

"Thank you, thank, you, you're too kind, thank you," said LaVie, trying to get the crowd to settle down.

"It's been such an honor to partner with Xycom, and especially to have a chance to work alongside my old QB from college, who made my passes easy to catch. Thank you, Mac. But without further ado I bring you my greatest achievement." He stepped to the side and motioned toward the large video screen, and the lights went dark.

Then a loud video appeared on the screen that immersed the audience in colors that blended into scenes of people wearing the Mindset while playing video games, driving, on dates, and in dangerous occupations. He continued to speak while the video played.

"Imagine a world that's safer, a world that's more connected, a world where you have more fun. Ladies and gentleman, I bring you the new Mindset for mobile, game consoles and computers."

At that moment three beautiful women and three

handsome men entered the stage from each side. They all walked in sequence and modeled the next generation of the Mindset. The camera zoomed in to show a close-up of the new device on the screens behind the stage. The crowd again applauded and LaVie lifted his arms to get them even louder. After the audience quieted down the spotlight returned to LaVie.

"It's been my goal in life to help the world become a better place; that's why today I am here to say that I will be leaving the technology world for a short while," said LaVie.

"What's he up to?" Jack whispered to Grace.

"Ladies and gentleman, I am announcing today that I just received enough petitions in every state to run as an independent candidate for the Presidency of the United States for this upcoming November election. So please raise your glasses to toast the launch and success of Mindset and my new future as President of the United States of America," shouted LaVie, but this time the light around everyone's Mindset pulsated at the same rate, and the crowd went absolutely crazy chanting, "President LaVie, President LaVie, President LaVie."

"Is he nuts? There's only six weeks left to Election Day; that's impossible, all states have deadlines," he whispered to Grace.

"Well he did it somehow Jack. Anyways, so what?

What's wrong with that? We need a President that understands business. Why are you so jealous of him?" she asked.

"Jealous? I'm not jealous. He just took credit for my invention, Grace; why would you take his side?" Jack snapped back.

"I'm not taking sides; besides, why do you care? You were paid millions for it, and you're not even wearing the Mindset," she said.

"That's not the point, Grace," Jack replied.

"Then what is the point? Are you ever going to be happy?" she snarled.

"When I get the respect I deserve, especially from my wife," he yelled, and then he realized everyone was now looking at him.

"Wow, you really can't just enjoy the moment, you bastard." She started to cry and moved away from him.

Knowing he'd messed up, he yelled, "Wait, wait, I didn't mean that," but it was too late and the damage was done.

As Grace backed up, she bumped into LaVie who had just conveniently come down from the stage.

Crying, Grace asked, "Can someone please take me back to the hotel? I've had enough for one night."

"Sure, I will, Grace. What's the matter?" asked LaVie, staring at Jack with those piercing dark eyes.

"You're not going anywhere with her, you son of a bitch." Jack lunged at LaVie, knocking over one of the cocktail tables and sending LaVie and Grace to the ground.

Monique snapped her fingers and within seconds security had surrounded the area and tackled Jack.

As LaVie helped Grace up, he yelled, "What's wrong with you? Are you crazy, Jack?" Then LaVie and Grace exited out the side door together.

"Really Jack, what's wrong with you?" said Paul while Charles and their wives shook their heads in disgust.

The security aggressively and embarrassingly picked Jack up and carried him through the crowd, out the door, and down the elevator to an empty basement storage room.

"Now what, are you going kill me?" said Jack to the guards.

"No Mr. Cooper, you couldn't be that lucky," replied the guard as he cracked his knuckles. The guards then proceeded to give Jack the worst thrashing of his life. When they finally finished, they dragged his bleeding body up to the main floor and across the marble front lobby floor, where they threw him out the front door onto the concrete. There he lay, staring up at the night sky. His tuxedo was ripped to shreds and covered with blood and wine.

As he lay there, he had just enough energy to murmur, "What in hell just happened to me?"

Chapter Eleven

The next morning Jack awoke lying in his hotel room, wondering how he got there. His body felt battered and bruised as he entered the bathroom and looked in the mirror.

"Where is Grace? I know I screwed up, but Grace would never have let someone hurt me. This makes no sense," he said to himself. "I need to call her."

He picked up his cellphone, dialed her number and waited for her to answer.

"Hello," she said.

"Grace, it's Jack," he said.

"Jack, I'm not ready to talk to you. I'm going to let you go."

"No wait, I was worried. I just want to hear your voice and know you're safe."

"Yes, thanks to Rob I am. He thought it best I not come back to the hotel, since you're being so violent."

"Violent? Grace, I've never laid a hand on you. LaVie is the one who's violent; he had his guards beat me."

"Are you really going to stoop that low, Jack? Rob wouldn't hurt anyone. You really need to get some help." She hung up before she started to cry.

Jack stood there speechless. His wife didn't believe he was beaten and trusted LaVie.

"This is not the Grace I know. LaVie must have

done something to her. I know. I need to call Paul. He'll know what to do," he said to himself and he dialed his number.

"Paul here," said Paul.

"Paul, it's me. Where are you? I need to see you now."

"Whoa, slow down, you owe me an apology first; you were pretty drunk and out of control last night."

"What? I had nothing to drink. LaVie was the one out of control."

"If you had nothing to drink then you need psychiatric help, my old friend."

"LaVie is controlling Grace somehow; she's not her normal self and she would never act like this."

"Hang on, first you accuse me of lying about Ming's, then you blow up and start a fight with LaVie after he got you over $100 Million, and now you think he's controlling Grace's mind somehow."

Jack stopped to think about what Paul had just said.

"What do you mean, Paul? I never said anything about LaVie controlling Grace's mind," said Jack.

"Err, that's what you meant," said Paul.

"No Paul, that's not what I meant, but it does make sense, you son of a bitch. It's the Mindset, isn't it?"

"No, there's nothing going on, Jack. I suggest you just go back to Michigan this afternoon and relax.

Grace will come around, and then you and her can enjoy some of the newfound money," rambled Paul.

"Whatever, Paul." Jack hung up the phone.

"Why is he lying through his teeth?" he said to himself.

He had known Paul for years and it just didn't add up.

"Maybe LaVie was controlling him as well. It's got to be the Mindset," he said to himself.

Jack started to think about the party; everyone had been wearing the Mindset except for him, LaVie and Mac.

Then he remembered the dream he had about the new Mindset building when LaVie was funding implanting memories.

"Was that dream warning me of what LaVie was really up to?" he said to himself.

Late that night, Jack arrived back at his home in Michigan. The lights were off and there was a light mist in the air. As he opened up the side door the air was stale.

"Well, no one has been home, that's for sure," he said to himself as he cracked the windows and then sat on the couch.

The silence was deafening so he hit the remote and turned on the news.

"Coming up next, see the new Thought to Text technology that hits the stores this week," the announcer said, as the news went to commercial.

"Wow, they don't waste any time, do they," he said to himself. Jack got up to grab a beer out of the fridge when the news report returned.

"Xycom is launching its new mobile appliance and app called the Mindset. This product is not only very slick-looking but also allows you to think and type directly into your phone, tablet, game console, or computer. It's great for safer texting and even writing emails. As a matter of fact, free versions were already given to all government employees and we're going to start using it here at the station," said the reporter as she placed the Mindset on her head to demonstrate.

"Please remember the Mindset hits stores tomorrow. I suggest you get there early because the lines will be long."

The news switched to the next story, so Jack muted the TV. He couldn't believe how fast they were getting it to market.

"It took Apple years to get the iPhone out, and Xycom did this in months," he said to himself.

Then he looked at the screen and there was LaVie speaking at some event. Quickly he turned the sound back on.

"And a vote for me isn't a waste. I'm not running to

take votes from the Republicans or the Democrats. I'm running to win," said LaVie and crowd went wild. Jack then realized, that all of the people in the audience were wearing the pulsating Mindset. As the camera zoomed out, he then noticed Grace, sitting to LaVie's left and laughing like nothing was wrong in her world.

At that moment the phone rang; it was Jack's daughter Emma.

"Dad, why is Mom on TV, and why are you not with her?" she asked.

"It's a long story and I'm still trying to figure it out, Emma."

"You're not divorcing, are you? I thought you and Mom were good."

"I really don't know yet, Emma. Just do me one favor: don't get a Mindset until I call you, OK?"

"Why? Brian is supposed to pick one up for me tomorrow."

"NO, don't, it's really important that you listen to me on this one. I don't think they're safe. They have changed them somehow and they affect how people think," he asserted.

"Oh Dad, you invented it; how dangerous can it be?"

"No you don't understand. I forbid you from getting one."

"Forbid? Really Dad, is this how you talk to Mom? Listen, call Mom and make up with her, will you? I'm going to let you go."

"Wait--" but it was too late; she had hung up.

"Maybe I am the problem," he said to himself and got ready for bed.

The next morning Jack logged onto his online bank account to look at the balance. His business account only showed his original balance. No transfer had been made.

"Those bastards never even transferred the money," he said to himself.

"Charles." He picked up his cell phone and dialed Scuttles.

"Charles here," answered Scuttles.

"You son of a bitch, you screwed me. There's no money transferred into my account," said Jack.

"Hello to you too, Buddy Boy. I would have thought you would have calmed down since the other night, but I see nothing has changed."

"Oh, a lot has changed, Charles. You see, now I have nothing to lose. LaVie took my wife, my technology and now our money," said Jack.

"Calm down," said Charles.

"No, you tell LaVie he just pissed off the wrong guy, Buddy Boy." Jack ended the call.

The blue light over Charles's Mindset then started to pulsate and he sent LaVie a message.

"Rob, I think we have a problem," appeared on LaVie's phone, interrupting his lunch with Grace, who was still wearing her Mindset.

Chapter Twelve

Nothing was making sense to Jack. *I need to get one of those new Mindsets, and get the frequency carrier analyzed,* and then he thought, *No, what I really need is Big Mike.*

Big Mike was a former Army telecommunications specialist and self-taught technology junkie who loved playing with HAM radios and satellite dishes, and rebuilding UNIX kernels for fun. Big Mike also had a thorough understanding of binary, hex, TCP, and a litany of coding languages and database architectures.

Big Mike was hacking computers before the word hack was even a term. Jack had met him his first year at U of M before Mike dropped out and went into the Army. Over the years he had included him on a couple of his tech projects. Jack knew that if anyone could find out what data the Mindset app was sending and receiving, it was Big Mike.

I've got no number for him, so I hope he's still living here in Royal Oak, he thought.

It was about 2:00PM when Jack pulled into the driveway at Big Mike's house. The home was a small single-level brick construction, built during the war. Jack climbed out of his Jeep, walked around the side of the house and knocked on the door.

After about a minute, Jack could hear someone slowly coming to the door. As the door opened he was surprised to see Big Mike's mother.

Wow, he still lives with his mother, he thought.

"Hello Jack, how are you, honey?" she said.

"I'm very good, Mrs. James. Very nice to see you," said Jack.

"Are you looking for Mikey?" she asked.

"Eh, yeah, I am," said Jack, feeling like a kid coming to his friend's house to play.

"He's downstairs. He never really goes anywhere, you know. Just sits down there and tinkers with stuff. I tell him he's never going to find a girl like that, you know," she said.

As Jack walked down the stairs he was hit by the smell of mold mixed with dirty clothing and pot. As he got to the bottom of the stairs he pushed open the door and entered Big Mike's domain. Everything was exactly the same as the last time Jack was there, over 5 years ago.

It's like going back in time, he thought.

The basement room was fairly dark with no windows. There were small lights that shown over the workbenches that lined three of the walls. Tons of disassembled electronic equipment, oscilloscopes, multi-meters, HAM radios, satellite dishes and even old tube style radios and televisions covered the benches.

The only things you could clearly see were the digital displays on some of the electronic equipment and three computer screens that seemed to be hooked to an old rack of servers.

Then, Jack noticed something move on the double bed that was pushed up against the forth wall.

Is that Big Mike? he thought as he slowly approached the bed.

"Big Mike, Big Mike, is that you?" he whispered, and at that moment Mrs. James had somehow sneaked down behind Jack without him noticing.

"MIKEY, get your ass up," she yelled.

"What Mom, what?" Big Mike said as he jumped up, half-naked.

Wow he looks bigger than I remember, Jack thought.

He wasn't really sure how Big Mike got his name, but it was probably due to his 6 foot 6 inch, 350-pound frame.

"You've got company," she said.

"OK Mom, who is it?" he asked.

"It's me, Big Mike," said Jack, and Mrs. James flipped on the main light.

"Jack, I missed you man. Where have you been, and Grace and your daughter--how are they?" he rambled while pulling on his pants, obviously very excited to see him.

"That's why I'm here, Big Mike. I need your help,"

said Jack.

"Anything for you man, you know that. I love you guys, but please stop calling me Big Mike. I'm not going by that name anymore," said Big Mike.

"Sure, sorry Big Mike--I mean Mike," said Jack.

"So what's up? Haven't seen you in a dog's age," said Mike wiping the sleep out of his eyes.

"I think I've screwed up bad, Mike," said Jack.

"No, not you, Jack. You've always had it together," said Mike.

"I think the Mindset is negatively affecting people's behavior. The problem is I just don't know why," said Jack.

"Mindset--shit, you were working on that 6 years ago. I thought it was just a gimmick," said Mike.

"Well it started like that, but it turned into something far more elaborate. The device actually worked. I partnered with an engineering team in California and they built an app to record and match what you type or speak into a phone with your corresponding brainwaves. After awhile, it learns, anticipates and reads your thoughts, and then converts them into text for typing on phones," explained Jack as he paced back and forth.

"Wow Jack, that's absolutely amazing. I hope you sold it for a lot of money," smiled Mike.

Jack started to say, "Not exactly, Rob..." but Mike cut him off.

"Not LaVie," said Mike. "You know that guy scares the shit out of me, dude. He screwed us both on RenTech, Jack. How could you do business with him again?"

"I didn't, Mike. Charles Scuttles and Paul kind of sold me out," Jack said.

"Charles and Paul? You've known those guys forever, Jack; they wouldn't do anything to hurt you," Mike replied.

"That's what I thought. I also thought that about my wife, but she's with LaVie right now, and my daughter's even taken her side," said Jack, now sitting on the bed with his head in his hands.

"Listen Jack, something doesn't sound right to me. I might not live my life right but I understand logic and what you're telling me is not logical," said Mike.

"That's why I'm here, Mike. I think it might be the Mindset and I want you to help find out what it's doing to their brains."

Mike was already putting on a shirt from a makeshift closet in the corner.

"Well, let's go get a Mindset," he said as he entered the small laundry room/bathroom.

"You will need to buy it, Mike. I need to stay off the grid," said Jack.

"If we're going out to the Xycom store, then I need to look good and get my breath smelling sweet," he joked and started to brush his teeth with an old tooth brush over the dirty laundry sink.

As they arrived at the Somerset Mall they noticed that nearly everyone in the mall was wearing the Mindset. When they got close to the Xycom Store the line to buy the Mindset was out the door and all the way down the aisle.

"Wow, this is worse than when the iPhone 2 came out," said Mike.

"They're at iPhone 7 now, dude, and Steve Jobs is no longer with us," said Jack.

"What, Steve Jobs is gone? Where did he go, Microsoft?" said Mike.

"No Mike, he past away!"

"Phew, thank goodness, I mean don't get me wrong, that's sad too," said Mike and they got in line. After about three hours, they finally made it to the counter.

"Hello sir, what size Mindset would you like?" asked the pretty young girl in a monotone voice.

"I'll take a double extra large," said Mike.

"Remember, I'm going to be using it as well," whispered Jack.

"Oh yeah, sorry. Just make it a large. Do they stretch?" asked Mike.

"Yes, they are virtually unbreakable. What is your Xycom phone number, sir?" she asked.

"I don't have one," said Mike.

"Unfortunately, you can't buy a Mindset device without a Xycom phone account. Would you like to start one?" she asked.

At this point both Jack and Mike already wanted to get out of there.

"Just give me the crappiest iPhone and the large Mindset," said Mike.

"Do you want Apple Care?" she asked.

"NO, no one cares about Apple Care," replied Mike, obviously frustrated.

"Sorry, sir. Can I see your driver's license, sir?" she said.

"Sure." He handed her an expired license. "Sorry, don't really get out to drive much these days, but I can't wait to try out my Mindset," he smiled awkwardly.

"Just wait, sir, while I activate your phone; also, I need you to create a Mindset cloud account so the app and the device will work," she said and handed him a tablet.

Jack watched while Mike entered someone else's account information.

"Thank you, sir, that will be $509.33," she said.

Jack counted out $600 cash and handed it to Mike,

and he, in turn, handed it to her.

"Thank you, sir; here is your change, your new phone and Mindset," she said.

"Thank you," said Mike and they both left quickly.

As they walked out of the mall, Jack looked over at Mike and asked, "So Mike, whose name exactly was on that old driver's license? I know you've never had a license."

"Let's just say I'm the original hacker and we won't be tracked by LaVie, Jack," and he smiled.

After the short drive back to Big Mike's house, he jumped out of the car and ran down the stairs into the basement like a little kid with a new toy. He then proceeded to rip open the packaging on the bed. Looking around the room, Mike walked over to one of the long workbenches and, in one sweep of his large arm, cleared the top by pushing everything onto the floor.

"Good, let's get cracking." He immediately turned on the iPhone and the Mindset.

"Well Jack, I've got to hand it to you, this thing is definitely cool looking, but it would look pretty stupid on my big head," he joked as he tried to fit it over his curly haired, large head.

"Aren't you worried about the phone being tracked to this location?" asked Jack, feeling a bit worried.

"Don't worry, there's no cell signal that can

penetrate these basement walls. They're all coated with metal foil and fully grounded," he smiled proudly.

"OK, if you say so," said Jack.

"Listen, this is what we're going to do. First we are going to hook the phone to my wireless connection and use the Internet to track data," continued Big Mike.

"We could still be traced by IP, right?" Jack asked.

"Really, do I have to explain everything, Mr. Neuroscientist?" said Mike before realizing Jack was just worried about his wife.

"I'm sorry Jack; let's just say I have a mega antennae."

"What do you mean mega antennae?" said Jack.

"It's a couple of satellite dishes I converted to pick up thousands of Wi-Fi signals far from this location. Then I have a simple script that pings for open Internet access. The script switches to another access point at the end of every transmission, so tracking is almost impossible. It's the ultimate hacker's dream. Free Internet and no way to trace where it's coming from." He gleamed in all his glory.

"You're a genius, Mike; imagine if you'd finished University," said Jack.

"Then I would know nothing, like you Jack," he laughed in his deep voice.

Mike continued to hook the iPhone up to the

Internet and then turned on the Mindset device. He then logged into the Mindset app on the phone with the phony credentials he had used to set up the account at the Xycom store.

"OK, you're going to have to use the Mindset, Jack, while I analyze what's going on," said Mike.

"Yeah, I know; give it here," said Jack, as he reluctantly placed it on his head.

Mike took out a smaller device with two antennae that were hooked directly to an older UNIX computer.

"What is that?" Jack asked.

"This is going to analyze the Bluetooth signal and my computer is going to convert the signal into text, and then store it in a flat file so we can read what's going on. We are also going to read the Internet packets that have been sent and received from the Mindset phone app. This will allow us to know exactly what the Mindset device is doing."

"Perfect, let's go. Start the app," said Jack.

"OK, here we go," said Mike.

Immediately Jack started to get a slight headache and then it subsided.

"You know, it doesn't feel that bad, they must have improved it. Actually, it really makes me feel good," said Jack.

"That's strange; why on earth would it affect your

mood?" said Mike.

"I don't know but it seems to. It kind of feels like a coffee high, but better," said Jack.

"Let's train the system first, like the manual says."

"The Mindset provides a few paragraphs to manually text. That helps the system to learn your brain patterns and match them with certain keywords," said Jack and he started to manually type the words from the manual. After about ten minutes had passed, Jack finished typing.

"Done," he said.

"Go ahead, give it try; think of something to text," said Mike.

So the first thing that popped into Jacks mind was, *Maybe the Mindset is not that bad after all*, and quickly it appeared on the phone and also in the flat file Mike was monitoring on his computer screen.

"That all seemed normal, but the phone app also sent two encrypted signals to the Mindset right before you typed," he said with a puzzled look on his face.

"To the Mindset?" asked Jack.

"Yes, definitely to it," replied Mike.

"It's built to receive sounds for the headset speakers," said Jack.

"I don't think they were sounds, the size was too small, Jack."

"Then what is it?"

"I'm not sure yet. Let me ask you this, why did you send that message?" asked Mike.

"I don't know. It just popped into my head, so I said it to myself. It also seemed to give me a good feeling for saying it," said Jack.

"That's fascinating. Remove the Mindset for a minute," said Mike.

"Why? We just started," snapped Jack.

"Easy Jack, just remove it; you can put it back on in a minute," said Mike, now interested at Jack's sudden aggression.

"How do you feel now?" asked Mike.

"OK, but I really would like to try the Mindset again," said Jack excitedly. "It's very cool, isn't it?"

"Well, yes and no. Let's try it again and I'll tell you what to say this time, OK?" said Mike.

"Sure bud, whatever you say," said Jack, chomping at the bit to get the Mindset back on his head.

"I want you to type 'I think the Mindset is defective and is possibly hurting my mind,'" said Mike.

"OK." He started to think about what Mike had asked but nothing appeared on the screen and then he started to get a slight headache.

"Fascinating. Now trying thinking, 'I think the Mindset is awesome and is helping me grow as a person,'" said Mike.

Immediately, the text appeared on the phone and Jack started to gleam with delight.

"Isn't that awesome? It really works. Let me say something else," said Jack, all giddy.

"Sure Jack, say, 'I think Rob LaVie would be a lousy President,'" said Mike.

"Sure, here goes," and as Jack attempted to think, he shrieked in pain and Mike grabbed the Mindset off Jack's head.

"Jack, my friend, this is not a thought to text device. It's a brainwashing machine. The device seems to be sending thought patterns to your brain and somehow chemically reinforcing them."

"I understand now. Xycom must have a database of keywords and phrases that they want people to like and then they send thoughts just like message notifications on a phone. The only difference is that the Mindset is stimulating the nucleus accumbens, or in simple terms the pleasure center of the brain, at the exact same time the thought is placed into the Broca's area, which is responsible for speech and motion," said Jack.

"I speak geek, not Greek, Jack. Anyway, you were right Xycom is controlling people. The question is why?" said Mike.

"It's simple, Mike, it's all about the Presidency. He's going to brainwash people into voting for him. I knew there was no possible way LaVie could have gotten on the ballot for office so close to the election date. Especially with no real backing and as an independent," said Jack.

While Jack had been talking, Mike had been pounding on an old IBM keyboard, obviously looking for something.

"There, here are the IP's of the servers that the notifications are being sent from. If I do a quick lookup we can find out where they're located and who owns them," he said and kept typing. Suddenly, he stopped and his face changed.

"What is it, Mike?"

"The servers are at the Control Datacenter in Hyderabad, India and guess who the main investor is-- LaVie Investments."

"I knew it," said Jack with murder in his eyes.

"Hold on, so now you've confirmed what you already knew. The question is, what are you going to do about it? You can't just go in half-cocked and accuse LaVie; he's brainwashing everyone, remember. You got to play this smart for your wife's sake," said Mike as he grabbed Jack by the shoulder and sat him down on his messy bed.

"I understand, Mike. Thanks bud. I know. I need to control my temper; it's not like me."

"Jack, it seems the Mindset device can make you

angry and happy, depending upon what it sends you. You wore the Mindset for a long time, Jack. You combine that with your hatred for LaVie, and it's no wonder you got violent," said Mike. "Who knows when they started to send thought and pleasure stimulations? Shit it's probably been messing you up for weeks or months."

"How did I let my own invention turn into this, Mike?" said Jack.

"Now is not the time to worry about that, Jack; now is the time to stop LaVie, and I have a plan," said Mike.

"Really?" said Jack.

"I have a close Indian friend that worked in data centers all over the world. He currently lives in England. His name is Akash," said Mike.

"A close Indian friend from England, and you never leave the house," teased Jack.

"So I can't have friends?" he smiled.

"Anyway, how can Akash help?" asked Jack.

"I'm going to back channel chat with him and see if he knows anyone at that facility. All I need is a temporary VPN access key and I can get into their database server." He started typing.

"Then what?" asked Jack.

"After I find the database and the table that contains the notifications being sent out to the Mindset accounts, then I'll write a trojan to piggyback on the notification releasing cron, sending anti-LaVie messages right before Election Day."

"Trojan, cron--what are you talking about?" said Jack.

"Didn't they teach you anything in neuroscience, Jack?" smiled Mike. "A cron is a software utility in the UNIX operating system. It can be used for scheduling backups and other types of automated operations performed by the server. I'm going to piggyback my trojan script to be executed by one of those crons at midnight on November 8th. In simple terms, I'm going to change all the messaging to make everyone hate LaVie."

"That's genius, Mike," said Jack.

"Not only will I change everyone's mind about electing LaVie but I'll also reveal what he and Xycom have been doing with the Mindset," added Mike confidently.

"But Mike, the election is only six weeks out; how long do you think it will take Akash to get VPN access to their control datacenter?" he asked.

"You mean this, Jack?" He pointed to the screen that displayed an IP address, an IPsec User Authentication Password and a Shared Secret.

"What, already?" said Jack in amazement.

"I told you a long time ago, Jack, don't mess with

nerds; we run the world," he laughed.

Jack cracked a smile but then stopped and thought about how much he missed his wife and how badly he wanted her back.

"Mike, that's a great plan to protect the presidency, but I can't wait six weeks to get Grace back. God only knows what he's doing to her," he said.

"Jack, I can only imagine how you feel, but you have to think. If we act too soon they probably have a redundant system that they could switch over to and recover. Closer to Election Day they would have no time to try and recover; besides, that is when the press would have the largest impact. It's all timing."

Jack knew Big Mike was right. If they tried to bring the server down too soon it would be easy for Xycom to cover up and switch to a redundant cloud farm and control the media response through the Mindset.

"OK Mike, how do we know they don't have redundant servers sending notifications out right now?"

"They probably do; that's why we're going to hack the primary database, which is usually replicated to other slave databases around the world. Once I hack in, I can easily tell which server contains the primary database. I only need to change the records on the primary and let replication do the rest for me," said Mike.

"Dude, you are an absolute genius. I sure hope this

works," said Jack.

"It will work, Jack, just leave it up to me. You go get some rest and let me work on this tonight. I'll get it all set up and ready to launch right at midnight EST November 8th," said Mike.

Jack agreed and gave Big Mike a man hug and walked up the stairs to leave.

"Take care, Mrs. James," Jack yelled up to the main floor.

"You too, Jack, it was great to see you again," she said and he left the house to return home.

Chapter Thirteen

As Jack got into the house he turned on the TV. The first thing that came on was the news. LaVie was speaking to a crowd with the caption reading "Live from Philadelphia, PA." Jack couldn't hear because the sound was muted.

"OK, let's hear what this jerk is saying today," he said to himself as he clicked the up volume button.

"…and let me make the message clear. I will lower taxes, balance the budget, fix this medical nightmare and stop terrorism in my first four years of office. I guarantee it, and in Washington no one gives a guarantee because they can't, but I'm not from Washington and I will," said LaVie as he pounded his fist on the podium. The crowd erupted in cheers and repetitive chants of "LaVie."

The announcer then came on and said, "Mr. LaVie will be in Philadelphia for the next three days for several rallies. The locations of these events are on his website at LaVieForPresident.com."

The camera panned around the crowd and Jack could see that everyone was wearing the Mindset. Then he noticed Grace sitting just off the stage holding her head like she was having a severe headache.

"That's Grace, and she's fighting it. That's my girl. I knew it; her mind is too strong," he said, but then LaVie came down from the stage and touched her chin.

She removed her hands from her head and the pain on her face seemed to go away. LaVie leaned over and said something in her ear and she smiled back at him.

"That's it. I can't just sit and wait while I know Grace is controlled by that demon. I have got to go get her now," he said angrily and turned on his PC to check LaVie's website.

"I need to stay calm, I need to stay calm," he repeated to himself as he read the website.

"OK, today is October 2nd and he's going to be at the National Constitution Center on the 4th. If I pick up Big Mike in the morning, we'll be there in 8 hours," he said to himself. He went upstairs to pack and then tried to rest.

After hours of tossing and turning, Jack got up just before the alarm hit 7:00AM. Without even taking a shower, he grabbed his bag and headed out the door to Big Mike's.

As Jack arrived, he saw Mrs. James putting out the garbage.

"Hi Mrs. James, is Mike up?" said Jack.

"Up? I don't think he's even gone to bed yet, Jack. Go right in," she laughed.

As Jack walked downstairs, he saw Big Mike now sitting front of four screens that he had obviously set up over the night. He seemed far more organized and more focused than the day before.

"What's up, Mike?" said Jack.

"Shhhhh, I'm almost done," he said.

"The program?" Jack asked.

"It took longer than I thought, Jack. The primary database was highly encrypted. I've been using over 100 clustered computers to crack the code and it took most of the night. Now I am just configuring my new little anti-LaVie notification scheduler. He's going to hate this, Jack," said Mike.

"Mike, I need your help," said Jack.

"I know, you said that already. That's why I've been up all night. What the heck do you think I've been doing here?"

"No, that's not what I mean. I want to go and get Grace, today in Philadelphia."

"No, no, that's not a good idea. We talked about this," said Mike as he got up and started to pace.

"I saw her last night on TV. She's trying to fight it, Mike. It's giving her headaches and I think that's what happens when you don't agree with what the Mindset is putting in your head." Jack stopped and a tear came out of his eye. "Plus, I can see it in her eyes; she's trapped, Mike."

"Don't do that, buddy, you know I can't handle

crying," squirmed Mike.

"LaVie is going to be in Philadelphia for the next two days. On the 4th he's holding a rally at the National Constitution Center. If I can get to her and remove her Mindset I might have a chance of getting her out," said Jack.

"Jack, not to be disrespectful, but THAT'S THE DUMBEST IDEA I've ever heard. You won't get anywhere near her or LaVie. He will have guards everywhere, especially looking for you," said Mike adamantly.

"What am I supposed to do then? I can't just leave her like this; I'll die trying Mike," said Jack.

"That you might, Jack, that you might," Mike agreed solemnly. "Listen, there might be another option. If I can find Grace's Mindset account in the database I could theoretically trickle real messages that allow her to see the truth. The problem is, if she thinks about the truth I'm sending, there is a possibility that the Mindset could read her thoughts and send them to LaVie." He started looking for Grace's account.

"That's a chance I'm willing to take, Mike; will you come to Philadelphia with me?" said Jack.

"Ha, ha, you mean you want me to leave Detroit? I'm not much of an agent type Jack. I'm just a computer hacker geek," said Mike nervously.

"Look, you were in the military and you love video games; this is your chance to be in one. Please, we've been friends for years. I need you," pleaded Jack.

Big Mike put his head down for a minute and thought heavily.

"OK, I'll do it," said Mike, lifting his head.

"You're awesome, bro," said Jack as he hugged Mike.

Then Mike realized he was hugging back. "Err, can we just stop with the crying and hugging crap? You know how much I hate people in my personal space, dude," he said and released Jack.

"Oh sorry, Mike, I forgot," said Jack and smiled.

"Listen, I'll locate Grace's account and download all of her learned Mindset keywords to a CSV file. Then we can start writing messages containing only her keywords. They need to be less than 140 characters, kind of like writing out a bunch of tweets," he explained.

After about an hour had passed, Big Mike had found her account name and they both collaborated to write out a list of eight memory insertions to be sent through the notification system to Grace's Mindset. The thoughts read:

1. INSERT @GraceCooper, it's Jack, I love you

2. INSERT @GraceCooper, it's Jack, I'm coming to

rescue you, I love you

3. INSERT @GraceCooper, it's Jack, LaVie is lying to you about everything

4. INSERT @GraceCooper, it's Jack, remember I love you

5. INSERT @GraceCooper, LaVie is hurting people through the Mindset

6. INSERT @GraceCooper, your thoughts are not your own

7. INSERT @GraceCooper, remember I love you

8. INSERT @GraceCooper, it's Jack, I'm coming to save you, I love you

"These are perfect, Jack. The love between both of you is key here. I will insert these thoughts into the database under her account name using another trojan script similar to the one I wrote for election day. The difference is it will insert all eight thoughts every hour to slowly change her reality to the truth. LaVie speaks from 7:00PM to 8:00PM Eastern standard time, so while he's speaking at 7:15PM, I will also schedule twenty messages to be sent every minute, telling her to go to the bathroom in the main lobby. There you will be waiting for her," said Mike.

"Yes, I will be, Mike, and you'll be my getaway driver," said Jack smiling.

"I have no driver's license, remember." He laughed

out loud and continued to change and schedule the notifications under Grace's Mindset account.

After Big Mike was done, he grabbed his old laptop and a bunch of clothes and crammed them all into an army knapsack and large cardboard box, containing all kinds of electronic devices and satellite dishes.

"OK, I'm ready to go, but wait, I need one thing." Mike reached over and grabbed the Mindset and smartphone they had bought earlier and threw them in the box.

"What do you need the Mindset for?" asked Jack.

"I don't, but you will or you'll stick out like a sore thumb. Besides, you never know; maybe I want to feel good," he laughed and they walked up the stairs carrying all the gear.

"Goodbye Mrs. James," said Jack.

"Goodbye Mom," said Mike.

"Where are you going, Mikey?" she asked.

"To Philadelphia to help Jack, Mom," he answered.

"I hope you meet a nice girl there," she said.

"Thanks Mom, see you in a couple of days," he said and they climbed into Jack's Jeep Grand Cherokee for the eight to nine hour drive to Philadelphia.

Chapter Fourteen

Grace gazed out the window at Philadelphia's historic city skyline from the Ritz-Carlton presidential suit.

She could vaguely hear conversation in the adjacent room through the half open door. LaVie stood at the bar, mixing a drink with Mac. Both were laughing and talking just softly enough so Grace couldn't hear what they were saying.

As she turned back to the window, the blue light on her Mindset started to pulsate. It was the reception of the first notification that Mike and Jack had scheduled. As she stared out over the city, she started to smile as the Mindset reinforced the notification by stimulating her brain's pleasure center.

I love you too, Jack, she thought and her mind started to clear.

What are they talking about in the other room? she thought. That was the first thought of her own, since putting on the Mindset at the Xycom party. Curious, she got up and started to walk toward the open door, just out of their line of sight.

"I can't believe it, Rob; you're going to be President. I can feel it in my bones," he smiled.

"Not just me--what about you Mac, my Vice President and the founder and CEO of Xycom, the largest telecommunications company in the world?"

said LaVie.

"I know, it's great to be working with you again, Rob. It seems like old times back on the gridiron," said Mac.

"That was a great year, Mac. I told you that day that you would do great things in your career, remember?" said LaVie, giving Mac a flashback to that moment on the field when Green broke his leg.

"You were such a great receiver, Rob, and a crazy SOB. Even though I hated Phil Green, it was tough seeing him break his leg that day," said Mac.

"Green was weak and it had to be done. I heard he's even a pastor now," LaVie scoffed.

"I always wondered how you knew that was going to happen Rob; it was like a prophecy," said Mac.

"I've always had that ability to sense the future. That's how I knew you'd be a success, Mac," said LaVie.

"I have to say, adding memory implanting to the Mindset was a stroke of genius on your part, Rob. Does anyone else know its potential?" asked Mac.

"Charles and Paul, but they are also weak and I'm easily controlling them with the Mindset. The only problem is Jack," said LaVie.

"Why is he a problem?" asked Mac.

"Jack is different, and I don't know why. His mind

is strong, Mac. Every time we've tried memory insertions on him, he got severe headaches and immediately ripped off the Mindset way before the thoughts could take hold. That's why we needed Grace- -something to keep him in check until after the elections," said LaVie.

"Can't we just have him terminated?"

"After the election I will get rid of him, but in the meantime I don't want any negative press around Xycom or the Mindset, and deaths always seem to stir up the pot."

Grace then entered the room and stood there at the door, staring.

"Why do you want to terminate Jack?" she asked.

"Err, that's not what he said, dear," said LaVie, glaring at Mac. "Just go back into the other room; everything is OK."

"No Rob, I heard you both clearly. You said you'd get rid of Jack after the election," she said.

"No, you're getting confused, dear. Sit down; it has been a long trip here," he said.

"I'm not confused. I want to know why you would hurt my husband, the man who invented your technology, Rob," she said, now starting to be more aggressive.

"Hold on dear, I'll explain in a minute," he said and he grabbed her by the shoulders, turned her around and walked her to the door.

"Mac, take her into the other room. I need to make a simple change," said LaVie and he closed the door. LaVie rushed to pull out his smartphone and put on his Mindset. LaVie had a master app installed where he could connect to any Mindset cloud and send memory implants to any Mindset just as easily as sending a text or tweet. Instantaneously, two memory insertions appeared on his screen, ready to be sent to Grace:

1. INSERT @GraceCooper, you misheard what Mac said about terminating Jack

2. INSERT @GraceCooper, Rob and Mac both love Jack Cooper and would never do anything to hurt him

LaVie then set the time-release schedule for every five minutes over the next day.

"That should be enough to fry her brain," he joked to himself. He shut off the app, removed the Mindset, and re-entered the main room. The blue glow on her Mindset started to pulsate and she slowly calmed down, as though she had been given a drug. Then, she slowly moved back to the window, like she had completely forgotten the conversation.

Rob motioned to Mac and they both walked back into the other room and closed the door.

"She's very much like Jack. She is also more powerful than others I have seen in the past. It might be the bond that she and Jack share. That kind of love can transcend time and even reality, so I'm not sure how long we can control her," said LaVie.

"What do you need me to do, Rob?" said Mac.

"We might need another insurance policy, Mac," said LaVie. He then leaned over and quietly whispered, "Get Jack's daughter, Emma."

"Will do, Rob; you can count on me, brother," said Mac.

"I know, Mac. I know I can," smiled LaVie.

Chapter Fifteen

As they drove down through Ohio, Jack turned on a satellite news station trying to get any current news on LaVie. After listening to back-to-back commercials about the new Xycom Mindset and LaVie for President, the news reporter came on and said, "News alert: people are starting to get slight headaches from using the Mindset. Xycom disputes the allegations that the Mindset is dangerous, and the National Medical Association and International Testing Association both agree that the Mindset is no more dangerous than any other Bluetooth headset device."

As Jack turned down the radio he said, "I just can't believe it. Xycom and LaVie seem to have everyone in their back pocket," said Jack.

"It's a powerful technology, Jack," replied Mike leaning way back in the passenger seat, trying to relax.

"The scary thing is, I invented it," said Jack.

"Hate to break it to you Jack, but it started way before you. People have been using brainwashing techniques in marketing and advertising for years; this is just the next generation. But don't you worry, it will fall like all the other schemes," he said.

"But Xycom and LaVie for president seem to own most of the media ad spots right now. I've never seen a politician and a company dominate so quickly, have you?"

"How about German manufacturers and its links with Hitler and the Nazi regime during World War II?" Realizing the shocking similarity, they glanced at each other for a moment. As they continued to drive, they sat silent thinking about the magnitude of what they were about to do.

Around 7:30PM they arrived in the northern outskirts of Philadelphia. Jack was whipped from driving and Big Mike was wide-awake, looking out the window like a little kid on his first vacation. All Jack could think about was Grace and whether their memory implants were working to help change her mind. As they drove down I-676, they exited onto Vine.

"Hey look there's a local Campaign HQ for LaVie," said Big Mike as they turned south onto N 15th St. and headed toward Race St.

"There it is, Jack, the Awesome Days Inn. It's a modern palace, Jack," said Mike.

"You definitely don't get out much do you, Mike?" teased Jack. "All I know is that I really need get some rest before tomorrow."

"You're going to need it, my little buddy, you're going to need it."

As they unloaded the Jeep they both looked up at the sky; the sun was about to set. The fall air was brisk and leaves were starting to fall from the few trees by the hotel.

"Grace always loved these types of days, Mike," said Jack.

"Listen, you'll get her back. Go lay down and I'll get my gear operational," said Mike.

"Why, what else are you working on?"

"Let's just say it's a surprise, Jack." He smiled and carried the box of equipment into the hotel lobby while Jack carried the luggage.

"Here, I got you water," said Mike and handed him a bottle.

"Thanks bud, I am pretty thirsty," replied Jack.

The next morning, Jack woke around noon thanks to the sedative Big Mike has slipped into the water.

Today's the day I get her back, he thought as he sat up on the edge of the bed and looked at Big Mike snoring in the other bed. He then started to look around the room. He noticed all the gear Mike had brought. There were several large antennae, an older PC, and what seemed like an old Xbox and a PlayStation connected by a network of wires and hubs.

"What in the blazes has he been up to all night? Not gaming...and I thought I was a geek," he said to himself as he noticed the Call of Duty game case sitting next to the equipment.

After Jack got out of the shower he walked into the sleeping area where Mike was up and already playing Call of Duty.

"Mike, what the hell are you doing?" said Jack. He then realized Mike couldn't hear him because he was wearing an old headset and microphone.

"Mike," he yelled again as he hit him on the arm.

"What? I'm busy; can you give me a minute?" He continued to play.

"Seriously, Mike, you do remember what's going on today, right?" said Jack, pulling off Mike's headset.

"What, what?" said Mike.

"I said, do you remember what we're here for?" said Jack, obviously upset.

"Of course I remember, Jack, I'm just getting ready for it and trying to relax. Don't worry, it will go well," said Mike.

"I am worried, Mike. Grace is all I can think about, and I have got to get her away from him," said Jack, almost in tears.

"Listen, I know she's not my wife, but this is no time for emotion. This is the time for logic and planning."

"It's not time for video games, either," said Jack.

"Don't worry about me, Jack. The only way to beat someone like LaVie is with a better scheme. Yes, he is a snake and you know that, but he is not as smart as you or I, which means we can win.

"I know but LaVie seems to be holding all the

cards," said Jack.

"I remember you being strong in your faith; what happened?"

"Life happened, Mike; that's what happened," said Jack.

"Listen I'm no Bible scholar, but one thing I remember from my old Army chaplain is that if God is for us then who can be against us, right?" replied Mike.

"That is true," said Jack

"Then let's pray and then get planning," said Mike. For the first time in many years they both bowed their heads and asked for clarity, guidance and the successful retrieval of Grace.

"OK, you asked me to help and now I ask you to please do what I say. I'm not the one going into the building, Jack, so I need you to be focused and not emotional. There will be no time for hugs and kisses when you see her--do you understand?" said Mike seriously.

Jack had never seen this side of Big Mike before. He knew he had some military experience but Mike had never talked about it, but at that moment Mike seemed different, focused, committed, and very military.

Now a lot calmer, Jack said, "OK, but since when did you become the superhero-type big fella?"

"There's a lot you don't know about me, Jack," he smiled. "Now listen up, because here's the plan: it's simple. Remember, I'm going to drop you off a few blocks away from the National Constitution Center at 18:00 hours. You're going put on this shirt and ball cap and hand out these LaVie for president stickers."

"Where the hell did you get these from?" asked Jack.

"Let's just say I went for a walk last night when you were sleeping. I made some new friends at the local LaVie campaign office. Nice people, actually. Young folks wanting to change the world," said Mike sarcastically.

"I bet," said Jack.

"You will also need to wear the Mindset," said Mike.

"Does it need to be on?"

"Of course, you'd be the only person there not using one, and also put these on," and Mike tossed him a set of nerdy framed glasses.

"Are you serious, Mike?" said Jack.

"One hundred percent. Put everything on. I want to see what you look like."

Jack proceeded to put on the shirt, hat, glasses and the Mindset.

"It looks nothing like me," smiled Jack as he looked into the mirror.

"Exactly--you didn't think you were just going to

walk right in. He's going to be waiting for you, Jack," said Mike.

"Waiting, why?" said Jack.

"How did you ever get your PhD in neuroscience? Why do you think he's got your wife, Jack?"

"I don't know, probably to spite me for starting that fight and embarrassing him at the party. Besides, Grace is a good looking woman,"

"Jack, no disrespect to Grace--she is a beautiful woman, but LaVie could have had any woman he wanted. He took Grace to control you, buddy, and of course he knows you're coming for her," said Mike.

"That makes no sense. Why didn't his goons just finish me off at the Xycom party?" said Jack.

"Because that wasn't LaVie's plan that night, Jack. You were supposed to put on the Mindset and conform like the others, but you didn't."

"I guess I'm just lucky that it gave me severe headaches."

"Lucky? I don't know how lucky you've been lately Jack, but LaVie knows that for some reason he cannot control you. For some reason you're wired differently than all the others. Maybe it's because you invented the Mindset, or maybe it's something else; I don't know. But what I do know is that he will be waiting for you," replied Mike, and they both sat staring at each other in an awkward moment of silence.

"I'm sorry, Mike. I know the plan is important," said Jack and Mike pulled out a box from beside his bed and started to open it.

"Now Jack, put this on around your neck," and he handed Jack a LaVie volunteer badge on a lanyard and another box of LaVie stickers.

"They gave you the badge as well?" asked Jack smiling.

"Well, not exactly, but they're free anyway, right?" laughed Mike.

"You're unbelievable," smiled Jack.

"Now listen, you don't need to get close. Stay toward the back and don't go anywhere near LaVie. Right at 7:15PM Grace will receive the Mindset messages and she should come to the bathroom. You must be there waiting. Once you see her walking toward the bathroom, I want you to quickly give her the other ball cap and shirt. Last night I inserted two extra memory implants into Grace's Mindset account; therefore, she will already know to put them on. Got it?"

"How do know this is all going to work, Mike?"

"Look if this technology has been convincing all these people to vote for that jerk, then she should come running into your arms, Jack. Besides, don't give up on your love and your faith, brother."

"I won't and I'm ready to go," said Jack but he was

not feeling as confident as he sounded.

"Slow down there buddy; we have a few more hours till prime time, so let's go over the plan again," said Mike, and they went over the plan again and again.

Chapter Sixteen

As Jack and Mike pulled up a short distance away from the National Constitution Center, they saw hundreds of people wearing Mindsets and walking toward the building.

"Wow, it looks like a scene from *Time Machine*," said Jack. "They look like sheep going to slaughter, and look they all have Mindsets."

"I know it looks weird, doesn't it?" agreed Mike.

"Yes, it's crazy. They've only been on the market for a few days," said Jack.

"Listen, don't worry about that. Just like I said earlier, don't go anywhere near LaVie. Let Grace come to you. Remember, you're just another volunteer handing out stickers, got it?" said Mike.

"I got it, Mike, and thanks brother, I really couldn't do this without you," said Jack.

"I know," he smiled, "but you can thank me when we have Grace back, Jack; until then, it's time to focus," replied Mike. "I'll circle around the area waiting for your text. Don't use the Mindset; just send me a manual text when you're on your way out, got it? Oh yeah, don't forget to hand out these stickers; you got to look the part," said Mike and he handed him the box.

"Yes, yes, I got it, I got it," said Jack. He took the box and stepped out of the car onto the sidewalk.

"Take care, Bro, and I'll see you shortly," said Mike and he pulled away, leaving Jack standing there, feeling alone.

After a second he took a deep breath and said to himself, "I can do this, I can really do this," and started to walk toward the building. As Jack got closer he noticed the Preamble on the wall of the building.

"We the People of the United States, in Order to form a more perfect Union, establish Justice, insure domestic Tranquility, provide for the common defense, promote the general Welfare, and secure the Blessings of Liberty to ourselves and our Posterity, do ordain and establish this Constitution for the United States of America," and then he thought, *Mike's right, this is far bigger than just Grace and I; this is about taking back our freedom. I can't let LaVie win.*

Jack continued to walk toward the front doors while handing out stickers. "Vote for LaVie," he said out loud while he cringed inside.

"Take a sticker, put it on your fridge and remember to vote on Election Day," he added and continued to walk up to the front doors in the middle of the crowd. As he entered the front doors, there was the smell of burning incense.

What is that smell? he thought. *It smells like incense, similar to my old church.*

Stationed at the front doors were two men dressed

in black suits, along with several police officers. A police car was also parked directly in front on the sidewalk with lights flashing.

"I thought there would have been a lot more security," he said to himself as he scanned the surroundings.

The main room was large and circular. On the side there was a balcony, which had stairs that gave access on both sides. On the balcony was a podium with about fifteen to twenty people directly behind it. They were all wearing Mindsets and held signs reading 'LaVie for President!'

A master of ceremonies then moved behind the podium overlooking the packed crowd from the balcony and, without saying a word, quickly got the crowd's attention. As Jack continued to scan the crowd he noticed that they all just stared up at the podium and waited, like they were in some sort of trance.

Strange, no one is even looking down at their smartphones. LaVie must be controlling them via their Mindsets, Jack thought.

As the time got closer to 7:00PM, more people poured into the main area. As Jack got closer to the front, he remembered what Mike had said about staying away from LaVie.

I need to find the bathrooms, he thought and started down the corridor against the flow of the crowd. As he turned the corner he saw the sign for the bathroom and leaned against the wall to take a deep breath.

I wish this was over, he thought. As he stood there, one of the men dressed in black suits noticed Jack and started to move toward him.

"So, you working hard?" the man asked in a firm tone.

"Err, yeah, I am. He's a great man," Jack said nervously.

"Mr. LaVie is going to change this country, sir, and put us back on the right track," he said confidently.

"I'm sure he is. I really can't wait," said Jack not very reassuringly.

"He's about to start speaking. You really should move back to main area, sir," said the man.

"Yeah ok, sure I will," said Jack remembering what Mike told him not to do.

"Well let's go, sir. I'm closing up this door. Mr. LaVie is just about to start." He put his hand on Jack's shoulder and moved him toward the event.

Oh crap, he thought. *This is not the plan. I need to stay by the bathrooms.*

As the man moved Jack into the main area he said, "You're a worker. Would you like to get up front?"

"Err, no it's OK, I was stationed to work at the back," and Jack walked away from the man toward the back where it was standing room only. As he turned around to face the balcony, the room suddenly erupted in uniform cheers that sounded like something from the Nazi Germany era.

"LaVie, LaVie, LaVie, LaVie," they chanted. The synchronized energy of the large crowd, combined with that smell of incense, seemed to hypnotize. Then, as if out of thin air, LaVie appeared directly behind the podium.

"How the hell did he do that?" Jack said to himself in amazement.

LaVie then looked to the left as Mac and Grace walked out and stood at his side. Confidently, he then moved up to the podium and shouted in a thunderous and amplified voice, "My followers," and crowd got even louder and the energy seemed to pull Jack toward the stage like some sort of supernatural gravity.

What is happening? He doesn't even seem human, he thought.

"Thank you." The cheers and applause continued. "Thank you. Thank you. Thank you so much."

"LaVie! LaVie! LaVie! LaVie!" the crowd chanted.

"Thank you."

"LaVie! LaVie! LaVie! LaVie!" the crowd chanted.

"Thank you so much. Thank you. Thank you very much." The crowd started to quiet as he lifted his hands.

"I said to my team a couple of weeks ago, I am so fortunate to be representing you in this run for the President of the United States of America. Mac McConnell, I also want to thank you for being there every step of the way and also leaving your company to become my Vice President. I am so lucky to have such a loyal friend that goes all the way back to college. Thank you, Mac, for always being there."

"LaVie! LaVie! LaVie! LaVie!" the crowd chanted.

"Now, when I decided to run, many of you said I would never win as an independent. Actually, both the Republican and Democrat parties laughed at the notion. But here I stand today, rapidly gaining ground on them while spending a fraction of the money, with no lobbyist that I'll have to pay back in the future.

"I'm not in this for fours years; I'm in it for eight. I will finally fix this economic crisis and political gridlock that's left us wondering whether America still exists.

"We have some serious issues in front of us and the truth is getting buried under the lies and deceit of the other two parties. So if you're tired of listening to the squabbling, the lack of leadership and bi-partisanship, then elect me to end it all."

"LaVie! LaVie! LaVie! LaVie!" the crowd chanted.

Yeah, you're going to end it, all right, thought Jack.

LaVie continued, "But at the end of the day, you

will be the one standing there in front of that ballot ready to vote. You will be faced with the choice of change. You will remember all the bad decisions Washington has made on jobs, the economy, taxes and deficits, energy, education, war and peace. Then you will look at the ballot and realize it doesn't matter what party you choose, politics will be the same. Remember, your decisions will have an everlasting impact on you and your descendants for years to come.

"I want your choice to change the path of America. I want your choice to define a new future. This is a fight to bring back the middle class and reinforce our economy with new infrastructure growth and investment.

"I ran for President because I saw our country and our dreams fading away. As many of you know, Mac and I have built and sold many businesses, and this country was founded on small businesses becoming large corporations. Mindset is just one example of what can be done and I will run this country like a well-oiled machine that is accountable to your hard earned tax money."

Again the crowd went crazy, chanting, "LaVie! LaVie! LaVie! LaVie! LaVie! LaVie!"

Jack looked down at his phone and the time read 7:16.

"OK, it's time." He looked at Grace to see if

anything was happening. Grace did not seem to be responding and Jack was getting worried.

What if LaVie figured it out, he thought and he started to sweat. Then suddenly Grace lifted her head and looked around, like she was searching for someone or had lost something. Mac and Grace were now standing slightly behind LaVie, who was still in front speaking at the podium. Grace slowly backed up and whispered something to one of the men in black suits and he nodded. She then walked behind the partition and out the other side toward the stairs.

"It's working, it's really working," Jack said to himself excitedly. As he watched her get to the bottom of the stairs, he slowly moved along the back of the room and in the direction of the bathroom. As he got close to the doors of the hallway he bumped into the same man wearing the black suit.

"Hello again, sir, where are you going? Mr. LaVie hasn't finished yet," he said sternly.

"Err, I'm just going to the bathroom," said Jack.

"Really sir, I thought you just went."

"Stomach issues--bad sushi." Jack kept walking by the man. As he looked back, Jack noticed that the man's Mindset was flashing.

Not good, he must be sending a message to someone, he thought.

Jack had now lost sight of Grace and was beginning

to panic, like he had lost a child in a crowd.

"OK, slow down and think," he said to himself and continued walking over toward the bathrooms.

"Damn it, she's not there," he said to himself. "I've lost her."

Then he frantically turned the corner and ran directly into a woman, almost knocking her over. It was Grace.

"Do you know where the bathroom is?" she asked, not even slightly recognizing Jack.

"Grace, look--it's me, Jack," and he removed the glasses and she teared up. He grabbed the Mindset from her head and shut off the power, then quickly he handed her the shirt and hat and told her to put them on. Within seconds Grace seemed to be more alert. He wanted to hold her so much, but he didn't want to draw any attention. Then the man in the black suit walked around corner.

"Oh, it's you again, are you feeling any better?" said the man.

"Yes, somewhat. My coworker gave me something for my stomach, thank you," said Jack, and Grace nodded.

"Glad to hear that." He kept on walking and then he stopped, turned around and looked right at Grace.

"Do I know you, ma'am?" he said.

"I don't think so," she replied nervously.

"Strange, you look very familiar," he said and continued walking in the other direction.

As Jack watched the man's Mindset light blink he whispered, "Look Grace, his Mindset is sending a message. I think he's onto us; we need to go now."

Quickly, they both moved toward the front doors. They could still hear LaVie speaking and the crowd applauding after every statement. People were packed right up to the door and lined up outside all the way down the path. Jack and Grace continued to hand out stickers to people as they walked through the doors. LaVie's voice was even piped outdoors for the sea of people to hear.

"Grace, go to the left. Mike is waiting for us down the street." They started moving quickly towards the pickup location.

"Crap." Jack was looking for his phone.

"What's the matter, Jack?" asked Grace.

"I need to text Big Mike that we are here."

"Michael? You got Big Mike to leave the house?" she smiled in amazement.

Quickly Jack started to type the text, "I'm out at the pickup location; please come ASAP."

Within a second Mike replied, "I'm on my way."

Now panting, Grace and Jack kept handing out

stickers and watching the road.

Suddenly, LaVie stopped speaking and the next words Jack heard over the intercom were, "WHAT? THEN GET THEM."

"He knows Grace; let's move." They entered the road dodging cars and frantically looking for the black Grand Cherokee.

"He's got to be here Grace," Jack panted. "There, there he is." Jack could now see the Jeep and they started to run.

"We are going to make it, Grace." Right as he said that, they both felt as though they were being watched. As they looked back everyone in the crowd stood still like possessed zombies, just staring and pointing at them.

"It's their Mindsets; LaVie must have had a mass notification sent, Grace," and they jumped into the back seat of the car.

"Mike, they're onto us, let's go," said Jack frantically, but Mike just sat there typing on the laptop that was sitting in the passenger seat. As Jack looked up he now saw several men in black starting to run toward the vehicle. The crowd also started to move towards them, while still pointing at the car.

"Mike, what are you doing? They're coming; let's go!" said Jack.

"Hang on," said Mike.

"MIKE, NOW. LET'S GO," Jack shouted.

"MIKE PLEASE GO," Grace screamed, but Mike kept typing.

"Guys, please wait," he said sweating profusely from his forehead. The men in black suits were now only fifty feet away from the vehicle, all with guns drawn.

Jack looked at Grace and said, "I'm sorry, Grace. I love you." They dropped their heads, waiting for the inevitable.

Suddenly Mike yelled, "YES, get 'em boys!' As Jack and Grace looked up, a large group of armed men wearing army fatigues seemed to come out of nowhere and quickly circled LaVie's men.

"Drop your weapons now," one of the men demanded, and they obeyed.

The men were of all ages and heavily armed with shotguns or rifles. None of them were wearing Mindsets and they seemed to be very well organized.

"What's going on, Mike? Who are they?" asked Jack.

"The boys are here, Jack, the boys are here," said Mike as he put down the window to speak to a bald man that was approaching the vehicle.

"Good to see you, my friend," said the man as he leaned into the driver's window.

"Last time I talked to you we were on the Ghost Level mission," said Mike.

"I know, we kicked some butt that day, my friend, but it's time for you get out of here. We've got this under control," the man said.

"Thanks Dan, I'll catch you in the Duty," said Mike.

"Sure will. Now its time to move on soldier."

Mike put the car in drive, did an illegal U-turn and sped away.

"Mike, who is that?" asked Jack.

"That's my old friend Dan Storm. He's my boy; we have fought together many times," smiled Mike.

"In the Army?"

"Army? No," said Mike, laughing. "Call of Duty, Jack.

"Call of Duty? What do you mean, Mike?"

"You know, Call of Duty, the video game. That's probably not even his real name," mused Mike.

"So those aren't your buddies from the Army."

"Heck no, I haven't seen those guys in years, Jack."

"Who are all those men, and why didn't they have Mindsets."

"Seriously, do you really think Mindset has the largest network of users? I have been recruiting over Call of Duty since we got to the hotel. You have to remember there are a lot of military and cops that play that game." He smiled.

"You are unbelievable, Mike." Jack hugged him from the back seat.

"No touching; you know I hate that crap."

"Thank you so much, Mike," said Grace.

"You're very welcome, ma'am, and now it's time to get you to somewhere safe. I don't think we've seen the last of LaVie," said Mike.

"Why won't he just leave us alone?" asked Grace.

"Because Jack is the only one that can take him down, Grace," replied Mike, and then he turned to Jack. "Jack, I changed the trojan script to execute in about one hour. Everyone will know what LaVie is up to. All the Mindsets will turn to bricks and he won't be able to control anyone until they reinstall the servers. This should give us enough time get to the media and get the message out about LaVie and the Mindset control he has created. The problem is he's going to come looking for us, so we need to vanish for awhile."

"Mike, I'm sorry to have gotten you into this."

"Don't worry, Jack, we're all in this together. LaVie is a virus and needs to be stopped; besides, I was getting tired of sitting in the basement, playing Call of Duty anyway." He laughed.

Jack and Grace sat quietly, holding each other tightly as he drove.

As Mike looked back at the couple through the rear view mirror he said, "Try to get some sleep, guys; we've got about a 7 hour drive to the safe house. It's time to stay low until everything comes out."

Grace and Jack looked at each other, smiled, and then leaned back to finally relax.

Chapter Seventeen

"AAAAARRRRGGGGG," roared LaVie as two of his men entered the green room to update him on Jack and Grace.

"How can one man create an ARMY? WE ARE THE ONES CONTROLLING THE MINDSETS," screamed LaVie.

"Sir, we're not entirely sure; all we know is that we were quickly surrounded by what appeared to be very organized vigilantes. They let us go without harm."

"Where were the police?" said LaVie.

"That's the other thing, sir. There were no police anywhere in sight. Even the police at the front of the building disappeared."

At that moment Mac ran into the room with another man. "Rob, the notification system has been breached."

"What does that mean?" scowled LaVie.

"It means someone has hacked into the infrastructure and destroyed the notification database. We've got our team in India working on trying to restore it as quickly as possible."

"How long will it take?" screamed LaVie.

"Three days, max," the other man replied.

"THREE DAYS?" LaVie grabbed the man by the throat and lifted him right off the ground, with what appeared to be superhuman strength.

"Rob, PLEASE, put him down; it's not his fault,"

pleaded Mac.

"THEN WHOSE FAULT IS IT, MAC?" He threw the choking man to the ground and turned towards Mac.

"You know my secret, Mac," said LaVie.

"What secret, Rob?" said Mac now shaking.

"I've been waiting to rule this world for thousands of years, but the stupidity of men, like you, has always foiled my plans in the past. This will not happen again," he growled.

"You've been joking about that since college and I never took you seriously. I know you're a great leader but you're still just a man," said Mac, trying to laugh and smile.

"Really? Oh, I'm much more than a man, Mac. I've been tempting man since the beginning of time. However, this is the first time that I've been able to control everyone's minds so easily and so quickly, and YOUR COMPANY IS SCREWING IT UP." He started to walk away from Mac.

"I know, I know. I'm sorry Rob, but we'll fix it. We didn't realize the servers could be breached. The company in India guaranteed that it had 2056-bit encryption. That's government-level NSA security," he stuttered.

"You didn't realize! You didn't REALIZE! Maybe you're forgetting what's at STAKE here, Mac--only the Presidency of the United States and complete control of the entire WORLD," said LaVie sarcastically.

"I know Rob, I know," said Mac.

"At least we have Emma in our control," smiled LaVie.

"Err, not really, that's what I was going to tell you…"

"WHAT NOW!"

"I got tied up last night and well, I forgot to send the men over to pick her up at college."

"YOU FORGOT." He quickly turned back and grabbed Mac by the neck, lifting him up as though he weighed nothing.

"Who, who are you?" stuttered Mac, choking.

"I've had many names over the years, Mac, so why limit me to one," sneered LaVie and his grip tightened around Mac's neck. You could hear Mac's bones starting to crack.

"Don't Rob, don't, I'm your friend, your teammate, remember?" he pleaded, still choking from the grip.

"I am no FRIEND OF MAN," roared LaVie and with no effort, he crushed Mac's windpipe and threw his lifeless body on the floor. As LaVie turned he noticed the other man crawling toward the door and stepped on his neck, "And where do think you're going?" Without a thought he finished him off with a twist of his foot.

Then he turned towards the other two men in black suits. As though nothing had happened, he smiled and calmly said, "Well, it seems like Jack Cooper just committed a double homicide in his attempt to assassinate me. Get the police over here to clean up this mess and deal with that incompetent notification company in India."

"Yes, my Lord," they replied and they quickly left the room.

"I'll get Emma myself," he sneered.

Chapter Eighteen

It was about 10PM when they crossed the state border into Ohio. Mike looked back at Jack and Grace as they slept soundly in the backseat.

Boy, it's good to see them back together, he thought and a tear came to his eye.

As he pulled into the next gas station, Jack woke up.

"Where are we, Mike?" Jack yawned and leaned over to wake Grace.

"We just entered Ohio," said Mike. "We've still got another three to four hours to go."

"Where are going?" asked Grace.

"Detroit, my friends, to my dad's old house after he left my Mom and me."

"I didn't know you owned another house," said Jack.

"Yeah, we rented it out for a couple years after Dad passed, but I've been using it for growing the odd plant," he laughed.

"Plants, what plants? Oh," said Grace, who then clued in.

"We'll definitely be safer there than at a hotel. Besides, it's located less than ten minutes from the College for Creative Studies," he smiled.

"CCS…Emma!" smiled Grace.

"Mike, is there anything you didn't think about?"

smiled Jack.

"Thank you, Mike, words cannot say enough," said Grace.

"Anything for you guys, you know that, but no one that is close to you is safe until LaVie is behind bars. Jack, we need to go directly to CCS, pick her up and bring her to back to my dad's old place. There we can lay low until my mass notification releases the truth tomorrow." Then Mike got out of the car and started pumping the gas.

"I think he's right, Jack, there's more to it than we know. For some reason, you pose a real threat to LaVie. I could feel the hatred when I was with him," said Grace.

"What threat could I pose? I couldn't care less about him becoming President. All I wanted was to get you back and that's over."

"No, Jack, it's not over. I'm not sure why, but I can still sense what he's feeling. He's enraged, and not like a man, but more like a wild beast," she said.

"I think the Mindset has just left you with a residual memory side-effect. I'm sure it will wear off."

"I don't think so Jack. I'm scared."

Then Mike leaned into car. "By the way, do you have any cash? I don't want to use credit cards. I'm sure he'll be trying to track us somehow."

"Sure, use this," said Jack and he handed him a

hundred dollar bill.

After some time had passed, Jack and Grace were woken again by the sound of Mike changing radio stations, scanning for the national news.

"Sorry, we're almost there, anyway. I couldn't wait any longer. I want to see how fast the news is spreading about LaVie. He's going down today; I can feel it," said Mike as he continued to switch to different channels.

Then he stopped on a news channel, "…and coming up, the full details of the attempted assassination of Presidential candidate, Rob LaVie and the murder of his VP running mate and his closest advisor. But before that, here is a word from our sponsors," said the radio news announcer and a commercial came on.

"Assassination attempt?" said Grace. "When did that happen, after we left?"

"Not sure, but that's not the news I was looking for," said Mike.

"What should the headline say?" asked Jack.

"The last message I sent out to all the Mindset accounts was the truth about the Mindset and LaVie's plan to gain the Presidency by implanting thoughts. I figured that would be plastered all over the news by now."

At that moment the commercial ended and the news reporter came on again.

"The top national story of today is the attempted

assassination of Presidential candidate Rob LaVie and the double killing of two of his campaign associates. While at his political rally in Philadelphia, a man by the name of Jack Cooper entered the grounds with vigilantes and attempted to kill Rob LaVie by gaining access to the green room. Long time colleague, VP running mate and CEO of Xycom, Matthew McConnell was found dead, next to Joseph Kinsley, a senior IT consultant to LaVie," said the reporter.

Jack, Grace and Mike felt as though time had stopped. It was one of those moments in life, when something so traumatic happens that your brain can't accept it as reality and your body goes completely numb.

The reporter continued, "Both eyewitnesses said Cooper and several other vigilantes broke into the green room while Mr. LaVie was speaking. McConnell and Kinsley tried to hold them off from gaining access to the stage but lost their lives in the process. In a quote the very emotional LaVie said, 'It's like the Xycom party all over again, and now he's taken Grace. I just hope for her sake that she is safe.' Police and the FBI are on the lookout for a Black Jeep Cherokee. Jack Cooper was one of the developers of the Mindset and was disgruntled when he was let go from the project."

At that moment they arrived at the small, rundown single-level frame house with shabby siding, missing shingles and a detached garage. The driveway was a combination of crushed stone and dirt and made a loud crunching sound as the tires drove over the top.

Furious, Jack got out of the rear seat of the Jeep and slammed the door. The air was cold and he could see his breath.

"No, wait, that can't be all. What about the mass notification I sent?" said Mike as he remained in the driver's seat, listening to the news reporter switch to another story.

"Well, it looks like it didn't arrive, MIKE," said Jack through the open driver's window.

"Look, everyone's going to be looking for your vehicle now. Let me get it into the garage," said Mike and got out to open the garage door.

"The Jeep--you're worried about the Jeep? How about being accused of a double homicide? This was your plan, Mike, remember, your perfect plan. It looks like your plan has backfired on us. I knew it was too easy," Jack snarled as he paced back and forth, thinking about what to do.

"Hang on, are you saying this is my fault? Who came and got me out of bed to help you in the first place? I don't need this crap," said Mike, and he climbed back in the vehicle and pulled it into the garage.

"Stop it Jack, it's not Mike's fault. If LaVie killed Mac, then he's capable of anything. Besides, Mike's plan worked," pleaded Grace.

"How do you figure, Grace?" said Jack.

"Because I'm here with you, Jack, aren't I?" said Grace, which seemed to calm him down a little. Meanwhile Mike had stormed into the house.

"Let's go inside and talk this over with Mike. We need to focus on getting Emma," she said. As they walked up the cement stairs to the front door, Jack noticed the house number and read it out loud.

"2708," he said, puzzled. "I know that number."

Lights now flickered in the dirty broken windows as Grace opened the front door. As Jack followed behind, a black cat jumped up on the step and rubbed up against Jack's leg.

"Hey buddy, are you lost," said Jack. Then he thought, *Wait a minute, I've said that before,* and he entered the house.

The house was small, with a living room, a bedroom and a kitchen. An old couch sat against the far wall with an old wood stove to the right that Mike had already lit for heat.

The house seemed fairly tidy for Mike, but it had a musty pot smell.

"Hey, it smells like…"

"It smells like what, Jack?" said Grace.

"Back in LA…" said Jack, shaking his head.

"What?" asked Grace.

"Err, what is the address here, Mike?" asked Jack, feeling a little dizzy.

"It's 2708 Earle St., Detroit, Michigan, Why?" said Mike and at that moment the black cat came through the open door and rubbed up against Jack's leg.

Jack jumped and flashed back to the house the night he left the hospital in LA, when Charles and Chris found him.

"What's the matter Jack?" said Grace, now very concerned about the health of her husband.

"I've been here before. I remember the smell of the room, the address, and even the cat. It's all the same."

"What, you know Jared? He's a stray that comes here at nights. I take care of when I check on my plants," smiled Mike, and he picked him up.

"Look Mike, I'm sorry, your plan did work. The problem wasn't the plan; it's LaVie, and you're right, he's not going to stop. We need to go and get Emma now."

"Save the apologies for when we have Emma, but remember, this is very risky now, Jack. Either the police or LaVie are going to be waiting for us. You can bet on it," said Mike.

"I think we all know the risks," said Grace.

"Well, we can't drive the Jeep."

"Then order an Uber car," said Jack.

"You can't; they'll track your credit card," said Mike, firing up his laptop. Then Jack remembered creating an account with Peter Molloy's credit card and his email address.

"Wait Mike, go to Uber.com. I want to try something," said Jack.

"Type in username p.molloy@zeeteo.com, then password: 'whatismyname'." said Jack and Grace looked on.

"I'm in, Jack," said Mike.

"I don't believe it," said Jack.

"When did you get an Uber account, Jack," said Grace.

"It's a very long story and I'll tell you both about it later, but right now just order the cab." said Jack.

About 20 minutes later, a black sedan pulled into the driveway.

"It's here," said Jack, looking out the front door. Cautiously he approached the vehicle. As it came closer, the driver window wound down and the driver called out, "Hello sir, did you call for a car?"

Reluctantly, Jack replied, "Err, yes, I did."

The driver stepped out of the car, opened the rear door for them and they all climbed into the vehicle.

"So, where do you want go, sir?" the man asked.

"College for Creative Studies on John R, across from the Detroit Institute of Arts," Jack answered.

"I know the area well. I grew up just down the road from there. It's a great school, don't you think?"

"Err, I am not sure, I mean yes, it's a great school," Jack replied nervously.

"I'll have you folks there in a few," said the driver and he backed out of the driveway.

As they drove, they all sat quietly, praying that Emma would be there.

Chapter Nineteen

It was close to 5:15AM when they arrived at the circular driveway of the CCS dormitory on John R. Road.

"There you go, Mr. Molloy," said the driver as they climbed out. As he heard the name, Jack just shook his head in disbelief.

"Of course, that's the name on the account," he said to himself.

"Can you wait for us, we need a ride back to the house?" asked Jack.

"Absolutely, sir," said the driver.

They stood there for a minute, staring at the old twelve-story brick building. The air was damp and cold.

"This building is supposedly haunted, you know," said Mike.

"Oh Mike," said Grace.

"Yes, a girl died there, I heard," said Mike.

Not listening to Mike, Jack asked, "Does Emma still have the same dorm room as last year?"

"No, she moved. She's on the seventh floor, apartment 701."

701--why do I know that number? he thought.

"Yes, I've got it. I'll go get her." Jack started walking up to the building.

"Wait Jack, they're not going to just let you walk in," said Grace and she ran up beside him, with Mike following close behind.

As the three entered the building they were met by a second set of locked doors. As they knocked a middle-aged African American man wearing a security uniform approached the door.

"Yes ma'am, want do you want?"

"I'm Emma Cooper's mother. I need to see her immediately. It's a family emergency," said Grace.

"Yes, Mrs. Cooper, come on in." He opened the door and guided them back to his desk.

"Can you call her cellphone to come down?" he said.

"Can I just go up?"

"Sorry Mrs. Cooper, no one's allowed up without a student. But I'll get the RA to go up and get her," he said and he picked up the phone.

"Thank you," said Grace and they walked into the waiting area.

"Do you feel that?" whispered Grace.

"Feel what?" asked Mike, but he knew what she meant.

"That uneasy feeling that someone is watching you," whispered Grace, and they huddled closer together in the middle of the room.

"I've always thought this building was spooky. I dated a girl that went here once. She was crazy and always said the building was possessed by that girl that died," said Mike in an almost childlike manner.

"Only thing scarier than that, is that you dated a girl," said Jack.

"What? I dated a few nut jobs. No disrespect to you, Grace," said Mike.

"None taken, Mike," smiled Grace.

Then the RA came walking down the hallway with one of Emma's roommates, but no Emma.

"Where's Emma?" she asked.

As soon as Carrie saw Grace she smiled. "Oh hi, Mrs. C. I'm so glad it's you. I thought maybe it was the FBI again."

"The FBI?" said Jack.

"Yes, she went with them."

"When?"

"It was around 8:30PM. Emma and I were walking down to Woodward to get a bite to eat and a large black SUV pulled up. They had black suits and official badges. They told her what her dad had done and said she wasn't safe and that they needed to take her to you."

"What?" said Grace, and she looked over at Jack and tears came to her eyes. Jack put his arm around her and she wiped her eyes.

"It's going to be OK, Grace," said Jack.

"Listen Carrie, did they say where they were taking her?"

"No Mrs. C, but one of the agents left this card just in case any other family member came looking for her. It's right here." She handed Grace the card that read 'Agent Johnson' and had a phone number.

"Thank you Carrie, could you give us some privacy for a minute?"

"Sure, Mrs. C. I need to get back to bed anyway. Say hi to Emma," she said.

"Thank you, please take care," said Grace and they huddled around, looking at the card.

"Agent Johnson, I know that name," said Jack. He grabbed his head and fell to his knees in agonizing pain.

"Jack," said Grace as she tried to hold him. Then, as quickly as the pain had come, it was gone.

"These episodes are becoming more frequent," said Jack, still rubbing his temples. "I must be getting close to LaVie," said Jack and as soon as those words left his mouth, another violent headache hit him again.

"What is happening to you, Jack?" cried Grace.

"It's nothing, Grace, please don't worry," said Jack. It seemed that every time he felt the pain he regained more focus and clarity.

"I'm calling the number. We have nothing lose. I

am innocent, so if it is the FBI then they can help. If it's LaVie then I'm going try to reason with him. After all, I'm not a threat to him," said Jack.

"Reason with him? Are you crazy? There's no reasoning with a madman, and you are definitely a threat. He probably had Mac killed and that's where you'll end up as well if you confront him," said Mike.

"Maybe, but unless we call this number, we will never even get to Emma," said Jack.

"As I said before, Jack, we first need another plan," said Mike.

"Sorry big guy, but this time I have the plan." He stood up. "I'm calling the number."

"You're crazy, it's obviously a trap," pleaded Mike.

"You're probably right Mike, but without knowing where Emma is, then a plan really doesn't matter. This is like a chess game and unfortunately it's our move without being able to see the rest of the board. I'm going on faith," said Jack, and Grace smiled at him with all her love.

"Alright Jack, but you need to keep the conversation short and sweet. Your goal is to get the location and that's it, understand?" said Mike.

"Yes," Jack replied.

"I'll call the number through my VOIP app on my phone. I'll hack the dorm Wi-Fi; that way they won't be able to track us," said Mike and he started to push buttons on his phone.

"Thank you, dear," said Grace.

After a minute passed Mike looked up from his phone and said, "Alright, I'm online," and he punched in the phone number from the card Grace was holding.

"OK, I'm going to hit dial. Are you sure you're ready, Jack?" he said.

"Yes, do it," said Jack, and Mike pushed the dial button.

One ring, two rings, three rings, four rings, five rings...

"Maybe it's the wrong number," said Grace and as that left her lips a familiar and very distinctive voice answered.

"Hello, this is Agent Johnson," said the man. Jack was speechless. The voice sounded exactly like Agent Johnson from the hospital in his dream--how was that even possible?

"Err, this is Jack Cooper."

"Hello, Mr. Cooper. Good to hear your voice."

"Do I know you?" said Jack.

"Sure, don't you remember, Mr. Cooper? You and Mr. Scuttles contacted the agency about LaVie's hostile take over of Mindset."

"We did? I know your voice and your name, but I don't remember any hostile takeover."

"Listen, there is no time to explain. I need you to go to this address: 285 Iron St., Detroit. We have Emma there and we can also protect you and Grace until we come down hard on LaVie."

"How do I know you're not working with LaVie?" said Jack.

"Well, don't take my word for it: speak to someone you know," said Johnson and he handed the phone to what sounded like Charles Scuttles.

"Buddy Boy, I've been worried about you. Where are you?"

"We're close, but why are you here?"

"As soon as the Mindset servers went down it broke their control on me. So the first thing I did was contact Agent Johnson at the agency--you remember him, don't you? He suggested we pick up Emma before LaVie's henchmen came looking for her," said Charles.

Jack, still not convinced, said, "I want talk to Emma."

"Talk? Come on over and you can see her," said Charles.

"I want to speak to her before we come," said Jack.

"Buddy Boy, she's a little preoccupied. I promise you she's fine, just come over," said Charles, and Agent Johnson returned to the phone.

"Again, the street address is 285 Iron St., Detroit. We'll see you soon." He hung up the phone.

"I told you, it's a trap," said Mike.

"I know, but why would Charles be there?" said Jack.

"They're either controlling him with the Mindset or they're threatening his life. Either way it's not good. How do know this Johnson fellow?" asked Mike.

"I recognize his voice and his name, but it's from one of those dreams,"

"Oh please, no more crazy talk, Jack."

"No seriously, it was from a dream. I really don't remember any hostile takeover at Mindset. The Johnson I remember was the FBI agent that came to see me at the hospital," said Jack.

"Then you have been messing with your brain for far too long, my friend. I don't think you remember half the crap that's gone on at Mindset. LaVie probably found out about the agency and that's why he wants you out of the way. Maybe it's time to stop chasing pipe dreams with scumbags, Jack," snapped Mike.

"Guys, please stop arguing. I don't care about any of this. I'm going to get Emma, with or without either one of you," she said sternly.

"I agree, Mike; we can't run forever, and if Agent Johnson and Charles are telling the truth, then they can provide us with at least some sort of protection."

"Maybe, but this is suicide; you're walking right into their trap," said Mike in disapproval.

"Mike, we understand if you don't want to come, but this is our family."

"OK, OK, I'll go, but I don't have to like it. But I will say one thing: while we're driving to Iron St, you really need to try to remember everything that went on in the past that might be helpful in saving our asses, Jack."

"Understood, Mike." They climbed back into the black sedan and gave the new address to the driver.

Chapter Twenty

As they drove to get Emma no one said a word. They all just stared out of the window at the Detroit skyline, thinking about old times. As they arrived at the address it was close to 6:15AM.

"Here you go, folks, you're at the Ritz, 285 Iron St. That will be seven dollars, please," said the driver.

Jack reached into his pocket and took out a fifty-dollar bill and said, "Listen, if I give you a fifty, can you stay here for a bit?"

"Sure, I'm here to help."

"Thanks, man."

"No problem, I'll be here."

Jack handed him the fifty and they all climbed out of the sedan.

"It certainly doesn't look like a government building, Jack," said Mike sarcastically.

"No, that's for sure, and where's the door?" agreed Grace.

"I'm not sure; maybe it's around the side," said Jack.

"You're not serious, Jack--this has psycho killer written all over it," said Mike.

"I'm going in, with or without you, Mike," said Jack and as he started to walk down the side alley, Grace and Mike followed. The building was an old brick industrial building that had been painted white, and a strong smell seemed to emanate from inside.

"What is that horrible smell, Jack?"

"I'm not sure, Grace."

"I know what it is--that's the smell of iron casting furnaces," said Mike.

"How do you know that?" asked Jack.

"My Dad worked down here when I was young and you never forget it. It reminds me of the smell of smoked ham and tar," said Mike.

As they got closer to the back, the smell got stronger and they could hear the banging of metal, which made them stop.

"I don't like this, Jack. These buildings stopped casting iron years ago," said Mike.

"I know, I don't like it either, but I'm not leaving without Emma," said Jack.

"I hate to say it, but she might not even be here," replied Mike.

"She's here Mike. I can feel it," said Grace.

"We'll I'm not arguing, ma'am, so let's keep moving," said Mike.

They started to walk again and as they turned the back corner, they noticed a single door adjacent to a large bay door.

"Look, the door is cracked open," said Grace as she saw the light coming from the crack.

"This is definitely a trap, Jack. Are you sure you want to do this without more help?" said Mike.

"Yes Mike, I'm sure this time I'm going by faith."

"Faith...err, OK," said Mike, unconvinced.

Slowly Jack walked up to the door to peek through the crack. As he looked inside he could see several large pits of molten metal in the ground, with about a six-inch high concrete lip around the edge of each pit containing the bubbling metal. The room was dark except for the light from the molten metal, making it hard to see if anyone was working in the building.

Jack left the door and walked back to corner of the building where Grace and Mike were standing.

"Mike, you might be right, it seems like an old operational foundry."

"Jack, she's in there," said Grace.

"How can you be sure?" said Jack.

"I don't know, but please believe me, I can feel her fear," said Grace.

At that moment a floodlight shone down the alley and they dove around the corner so as to not be seen.

As Mike peeked back around at the source he said, "It's the police."

"The police?" said Jack.

"Yes, I told you this was a trap. There's no government building here, and now the police are here.

We need to leave."

"No Mike, please, we need to go inside," said Grace.

"Inside? Are you crazy? I hate foundries; they're hot and remind me of hell," said Mike.

"Well, I'm going in," said Grace and she opened the door and entered the extremely hot room.

"Mike, let's go," said Jack and pulled Mike by the coat and they entered into the foundry. Grace had stopped about five feet into the building. She stood absolutely still, staring at the molten pits directly ahead.

"What's the matter, Grace?" said Jack, slightly behind her.

"You don't see?" she replied. Jack tried to focus his eyes beyond the pits of molten metal. Then slowly his eyes cleared and the hair on his neck stood on end.

There hung Emma over the molten pit in some type of fireproof suit.

"God please, don't let this happen," she pleaded. Then Jack noticed Mike edging towards the far wall to avoid getting burned.

"Mike, where are you going?" said Jack.

"I'm going to try and get to the office. Maybe there's another suit so I can get her down," said Mike.

"Wait, let me help you," said Jack.

"No, you stay with Grace," said Mike and he moved closer to the back wall.

Then Jack noticed that Emma was rocking back and forth. "Mike, look she's moving."

Mike stopped and looked at Emma from his new position. "Jack, we have another problem."

"What?" Then Jack saw exactly what Mike was seeing. A man wearing plain street clothes was standing behind the frame Emma was suspended from.

"Who are you? Put her down and leave her alone," Jack screamed.

"So it's been quite the day so far, my old friend. I bet you didn't see that one coming," said the man, and he slowly walked into the light of the molten metal pit.

"Paul, I don't understand--why?"

"Why? Do you really need to ask that question, Jack? You and Grace have been screwing up the plans from the beginning. Do you really think you own the Mindset technology just because you think you invented it, you self-righteous bastard?"

"Please Paul, this is crazy; we've been friends for years. You've known Emma all her life; you were even at her christening," said Jack.

"Grace, come here and I will let Emma live," said Paul.

"Don't go Grace; he's not going to let her go. Not

to mention you'll die from the heat," said Mike and he stepped a little closer to Paul.

Then Jack realized that Paul was standing directly next to a molten metal pit without a fire suit.

"How are you able to withstand that heat, Paul?" asked Jack, but Grace already knew why.

"Because it's not Paul, Jack," said Grace.

"I don't understand," said Jack.

"It only appears to be him," she yelled and at that moment Paul's image changed into Agent Johnson, then into Charles, and finally LaVie.

"It seems she's got me figured out, Jack. I've been waiting to control this realm since the very beginning. Your Mindset was the key but for some reason you're the only person it cannot control. So if you want Emma back alive then unfortunately I'm going to need your soul."

"My soul? I don't understand," said Jack, confused.

On the other side of the room, Mike continued to move closer to LaVie, getting ready to push him into the pit.

Suddenly, three ear-splitting "BANGS" echoed through the room. Mike dropped and lay there on the ground, with two bullet holes in his chest and one in his head.

"NOOOOOO…" cried Jack. Then out of nowhere

they were completely surrounded by men in black suits, all wearing the Mindset device.

"Did you really think I was alone, Jack?" said LaVie.

"Do you really think we are?" said Grace defiantly, and she began to move toward LaVie and the intense heat.

"Please, you think your God is going to help you here, Grace? He abandoned you people a long time ago!"

"I will not be afraid of any evil-being claiming to be all-powerful. I want my daughter back now," she demanded and slowly kept moving.

"Grace, STOP; he killed Mike; he's crazy," said Jack.

"I am not just claiming to be all powerful, Grace. I am." LaVie reached over and aggressively pulled Grace beside him.

"STOP," screamed Jack.

Then holding her arms down by her side he said, "Well, it's been awhile since I held you, my dear; did you miss me?" He cackled and tried to lick her face with his snake-like tongue. Grace struggled violently, turned her face and then spat at him.

"See Jack, I can make anyone spit like a snake," LaVie sneered.

"Please, she can't handle the heat; let her go," begged Jack.

"Don't you worry Jack, while I'm holding her she can handle anything I can. You need to start worrying about when I let her GO." He swung her over the pit of molten metal with one arm.

"NO, you better leave her alone." Jack moved forward but the heat was too intense and he had to move back.

"Really Jack, or you'll do what? I'm the one holding all the cards now," and with his other hand he easily lifted Emma off the metal hook and held both of them over the top of the pit.

"You see, I have everything that you love in my full control, and like I told you back at Mindset, there's absolutely nothing you can do about it."

"OK, I'll do it, just let them go," pleaded Jack.

"Then deny your useless god and pledge your allegiance to me, and your realm will be mine forever."

"NO Jack, see the truth, your mind is the realm he's speaking of," screamed Grace.

"SILENCE," LaVie screamed and shook her like a doll.

"My mind?" Then he realized what Grace had said and a small light appeared in his mind and started to grow. As it became larger, it felt like someone or something had removed the blinders from his eyes.

Then he looked up at his wife and daughter dangling over the pit and he could now see this realm or reality for what it really was. Nothing more than a game of puppets played by a powerless puppet master.

"You have no power over them in this realm, LaVie," said Jack, and he started to move forward.

"Don't come any farther or I'll drop them both,"

"I don't think so," said Jack calmly, and he raised his hand and said, "I COMMAND YOU TO RELEASE THEM."

Immediately steam started to rise from LaVie's fingers where he firmly held Emma and Grace.

"WHAT IS THIS ILLUSION?" he screamed in agony as steam started rising from the rest of his body.

"IT'S NO ILLUSION," smiled Jack and the heat forced LaVie to stagger away from the pit, dropping Emma and Grace on the ground.

"GET THEM," he screamed to his henchman but as they moved forward towards the pits they burst into flames.

Jack now realized he was unaffected by the heat and he leaped at LaVie, dragging him to the ground, and they both rolled to edge of the molten metal pit.

"NO!!!" screamed LaVie in terror as he fought wildly against Jack's iron grip. But the more LaVie fought, the closer they moved to edge of the molten metal.

Then Jack looked back at Grace and Emma, now beside Mike's lifeless body, and said, "Forgive me, Grace, for not believing. I love you."

"I love you too," said Grace and she smiled and nodded, approving of what she knew he was about to do. Then without hesitation Jack looked LaVie right in the eyes and said, "It's time for a new mindset."

Jack rolled over, dragging LaVie into the pit, where the molten lake of fire consumed both their bodies.

Chapter Twenty-One

Jack awoke to a white light so intense it seemed to burn his eyes. The harder he tried to focus, the more his eyes hurt.

I'm dead, he thought. Then he noticed a sound quietly ringing in his ears that continued to grow louder and louder. He began to see fuzzy figures slowing moving on a white background in the distance and the sounds became even clearer.

"Those are people talking," he said to himself. "It sounds like Grace."

Slowly the figures started to become more vivid. Then he saw Grace sitting in the middle of what seemed like a circle of people. As his eyes slowly cleared, he saw his daughter Emma on her left. He then squinted and could now see Charles on Emma's left and Paul on Grace's right. Then Que and his wife came into focus on Paul's right, and a large man standing over the back of everyone.

Is that God? he thought, then smiled. *It's Mike; he's alive. But why are they holding hands?* Then he realized Grace was leading a prayer.

"Heavenly Father, I ask you now to protect Jack as he lies in this coma. We thank you, Lord, that Agents Johnson and Kloven just happened to be following Jack the night of the accident,

"We realize, Lord, that Jack's injuries from the car

accident are extensive, but we ask, Lord, that he recovers thoroughly and comes out of the coma with full brain function,

"We rest in your abiding presence, releasing every care and anxiety. Father, we also pray for the family of the other driver, who was killed in the accident,

"We know in the moments of pain we need you for strength, and we thank you for always being there, in Jesus' name, Amen."

As Jack listened to the prayer he began to recall the accident, the meeting at Mindset with Charles and Paul, the argument with Paul at Ming's, the black SUV that followed him down Western Ave, and the force of the impact as he turned on the I-10 ramp.

Then he heard Grace mention Agents Johnson and Kloven and Jack flashed back to the day they entered his ER room and gave him his wallet and keys.

By now Jack was fully conscious and as Grace lifted her head from the prayer, she noticed that he was awake.

"Jack, you're awake, thank God," she exclaimed as she jumped up and rushed over to hug him, with Emma right behind her. The three embraced and tears of joy flowed down their faces.

Smiling, Mike, Charles, Paul, Que and Que's wife stood at the bottom of his bed.

"Where am I?" said Jack.

"You've been in a coma for two days," Grace explained. "You have a lot of swelling in your brain, so Dr. Gamble was worried about brain damage."

Jack was still so fatigued, but his mind was gaining clarity. It was now becoming obvious to him that his memories must have been caused by the coma.

"I dreamt you and Emma were taken," said Jack, rubbing his head.

"By who?" asked Grace.

"LaVie," said Jack.

"Who?" she asked.

"No one, it's nothing. It was just a hallucination from the coma," said Jack.

"The brain is very powerful, Jack; you for one know that," she gleamed; overjoyed he was awake and responsive.

"It's so good to see you all," said Jack.

"I flew here immediately after Agent Johnson called. Luckily, they found your jacket and wallet at the scene of the accident," she said.

"Yeah, I know; I already met him," said Jack.

"That would be impossible, hon, you've been in a coma the entire time. You must have just heard me saying his name." she replied.

"No, he was with Agent Kloven. They brought me my wallet and keys," said Jack. Then he flashed back, remembering the name Peter Molloy on the driver's license.

"You must have heard me say his name, Jack," said Grace.

"Yes, you're right, I must have. Besides, it had the wrong name on the driver's license anyway. I'm definitely not Peter Molloy," he said, still rubbing his temples.

"What? Did you say Peter Molloy?" asked Grace, now stunned.

"Yes, why? Do we know him?" asked Jack. "It feels like we should for some reason."

"Jack, that's the name of the driver of the car that hit you. He wasn't wearing his seatbelt and died on impact," replied Grace in amazement.

"Jack, you must have heard someone in the room say his name," Paul added.

"But that would be impossible Paul; you see, I wanted to pray for the driver's family so I requested Agent Johnson to send me his name," she explained.

"Yeah, so Jack still probably heard you on the phone or something," Paul replied.

"No Paul, because I received his name in text only five minutes ago," Grace answered, and she held up her iPhone screen displaying the words 'Peter Molloy' close to 5 minutes ago.'

The room went into an awkward silence. Breaking the tension Charles said, "Well, the most important thing is that it's all over. You really had us worried, Buddy Boy."

Hearing the words 'Buddy Boy' gave Jack another headache that made him push harder on his temples.

"Are you OK, Jack?" Grace asked, concerned.

"Yes, yes, I'm good, just residual flash backs from those dreams. I just need to rest," he answered.

"We'll get the doctor in here to look at you," she said.

Then Big Mike moved up beside the bed.

"You don't know how good it is to see you again, my brilliant friend," said Jack, and a tear came into his eye.

"You know, I needed a reason to get out of Mom's basement anyway, Jack." They both laughed.

"When I get out of here, I really want you to come work with us, Mike," said Jack.

"I don't know about that. I hate California, you know that," he chuckled.

"Just think about it. We could really use someone with your talents," said Jack and he reached out to grab his arm.

"Hey, I told you before I don't like the touching." Everyone laughed.

Hearing all the commotion, a larger-sized nurse came in, surprised to see Jack awake and surrounded by all of the visitors.

"Why didn't someone tell me he woke up? OK everyone, I'm going to have to ask everyone to leave. Dr. Gamble will need to run some tests on Jack now that he is awake," she barked.

Then, switching to a quieter, more compassionate tone, she said, "Mrs. Cooper, you and your daughter can stay the night, but the others will need to leave, dear."

Paul grabbed Jack's hand, grinning, and said, "We'll see you soon, brother. We have lots to talk about at Mindset."

"Yeah, see you soon, Buddy Boy," added Charles, also grinning.

As the nurse checked Jack's IV she said, "Mr. Cooper, you just rest and I'll get the doctor."

Then everyone slowly exited the room. Emma kissed him and then sat down in the reclining chair. Grace moved closer and laid her head on Jack's lap and held his hand. Jack finally had a feeling of safety, peace and calmness.

Chapter Twenty-Two

As Jack lay there he started to feel very sleepy and his eyes began to get heavy.

"Why don't you get some sleep, hon? Your body still needs to do a lot of healing from the car accident," said Grace.

"Yes, I do feel tired," said Jack.

"Just close your eyes and don't worry about a thing. We'll be right here. I love you," said Grace, and she kissed him on his lips and then turned off the light.

"I love you too," said Jack, and he smiled.

This is definitely reality, he thought, and with eyes almost closed, he rolled his head over to get one last look at Grace and Emma before falling asleep.

They're beautiful, he thought, as he watched Grace rest her head on his legs and Emma cuddled up in the chair.

He then noticed a cold draft coming from the open doorway.

Swiftly a figure blocked the doorway with its back to Jack's line of sight. The room was darker than the hallway, so it was impossible for Jack to identify the figure. As he tried to focus his eyes, he felt the room became even colder.

"Dr. Gamble, is that you?" he asked the figure, but it did not respond. "Nurse, is that you? Could you please close that door? There seems to be a cold draft."

Then Jack felt as though the joy was being sucked out of his mind, and the hair stood up on Jack's neck as the figure slowly turned around.

"LaVie," said Jack.

His enemy stood staring with blood red eyes and a sickly pale complexion that seemed to glow without light. LaVie then scowled with his same terrifying look and without even opening his mouth he bellowed, "YOUR REALM? I'M NOT DONE WITH YOU YET, JACK COOPER!" He transformed into a cloud of fog that rushed over Grace's sleeping body, stopped in front Jack's face, and then quickly entered through his mouth and nose.

Jack grabbed his head in surreal pain and screamed, "NOT AGAIN!!!"

But this time it was different; there were no colors or hallucinations. Instead, he found himself standing back in his home lab, like no time had passed. In his right hand was his smart phone that read, 'Not much, you?' on the screen, right below where his friend Paul had just texted, 'Hey Jack, what's up?'

At that moment Grace walked into the basement lab. "Jack, are you coming back outside? You said you weren't going to work, remember?"

Jack turned to face her, his eyebrows wrinkled and his mouth gaped open as though he had just seen a ghost.

"WHAT THE HELL JUST HAPPENED?" he cried, and then he realized that he was still wearing the Mindset prototype. Quickly he ripped it off his head and threw it on the mannequin figure, like it was somehow possessed.

He then grabbed Grace by the hand and said, "I'm ready to sit with you." He smiled, closed the door to his lab, and went upstairs.

About The Author

Stephen Sadler was born in Nottingham, England in 1965. Apart from writing, he is the registered inventor for various technology patents in education, entertainment, engineering, and sports.

Stephen graduated Summa Cum Laude from Central Michigan University and has been honored with awards for technology and entrepreneurship.

On a personal note, he loves mentoring young entrepreneurs, coaching youth soccer, playing ice hockey, and spending time with his family and friends.

For more information, check out his website: https://stephensadler.com